CRIMINAL PROSECUTOR

The Flight From Yakima

Inspired by True Events

A Novel by Vic Kusske

Contents

Tijuana

El Rosario

San Carlos
Nuevo
Guaymas
Santa
Rosalia

Loreto Puerto
Escondido
Agua
Verde Topolobampo
San Evaristo
La Paz
Ensenada
de Muertos

Cabo San Lucas

PROLOGUE

B old words across the top of a poster being held by a Mexican Navy Captain declared: ***"WANTED BY THE FBI, NICOLAS JAMES CABOT*** *– Former Municipal Police Narcotic Detective wanted for Attempted Murder and Interstate Flight to Avoid Prosecution, Contact Interpol or The United States Federal Bureau of Investigation ..."*

The 25-foot Defender Class Patrol boat with the words "Rescate" (Rescue) and "Armada de México" (Mexican Navy) on its sides, powered by two, 200 HP Honda outboard motors and fitted with machine gun mounts fore and aft, moved slowly toward a point of land on the Sea of Cortez.

"¡Vayan a sus estaciones!" the captain ordered the five crewmen to their stations as they rounded the point and entered the small bay called Agua Verde (Green Water).

The tiny, remote village of about twenty families that subsisted on a harvest of fish from the Sea of Cortez was not a threat to those aboard the patrol boat, but the wanted man in the FBI poster warranted caution. Two lookouts aboard the Mexican patrol boat studied intently through field glasses a 32-foot sloop-rigged sailboat anchored in the northeast corner of the bay. "Just Dandy" was written on the aft quarter of the Ericson keelboat and a woman in the cockpit was observed looking at the patrol boat with field glasses of her own. Two Navy divers, outfitted in wet suits and SCUBA diving gear, launched an inflatable dinghy from the Mexican navy patrol boat. Powered by a 50 HP outboard motor, the inflatable paralleled the patrol boat as it approached the anchored sailboat.

"¡Persona en el agua!" yelled a patrol boat lookout as a man was seen entering the water from the stern of the sailboat.

The patrol boat approached the sailboat from its starboard side and the divers in the inflatable boat approached from the port side. As they got closer one diver noticed what appeared to be a person swimming under water into a sea cave at the shore.

"¡En la cueva!" warned the diver as he pointed at a group of several sea caves about fifty yards away at the shoreline.

It was high tide and the three caves next to each other were about half full of sea water.

"¿Cual Cueva?" the lookout was not sure which cave the swimmer had entered so the two divers rolled off their inflatable dinghy into the water and each took a cave, while the patrol boat contacted the sailboat.

Captain Hugo Chávez interviewed the female occupant of the sailboat, and a cursory search of the vessel was done. One patrol boat lookout manned the bow mounted M249 SAW light machine gun, while the other lookout closely watched the entrance to the three sea caves.

After a few minutes, the lookout yelled, "Sangre en el agua!" as the water at the entrance to the center cave turned red.

The captain immediately ordered the lookout and the sailor on the bow machine gun to suit up in SCUBA dive gear. Issuing SPP-1 underwater pistols to the two additional divers the captain took over the bow machine gun. The SPP-1 underwater pistol was a new development in the 1970's. It had four barrels that were smooth bore which fired steel darts achieving an underwater range of about fifty feet.

As the two new divers entered the water a body in a wet suit was seen floating lifeless just inside the entrance to the center cave. Both divers went as quickly as they could to the floating diver and when they reached him, they turned him over. One diver began giving him breaths while the other looked for the source of the blood that surrounded them in the water. After a few moments, the lifeless body was pulled into the patrol boat while the second diver submerged and entered the center cave with the underwater pistol in his hand. Ten minutes later, the second diver appeared at the entrance to the center cave and began swimming toward the patrol boat. He was assisted aboard and was terribly upset and speaking rapidly in Spanish. It was quickly learned both divers who entered the caves looking for the swimmer were dead. The first diver was killed by knife wounds while the second diver was strangled and hung from a protruding rock inside the cave. The captain had his remaining crew keep watch over the three cave entrances while he radioed for assistance. Spotlights were trained on the caves throughout the night, and the next morning two other Mexican navy vessels arrived. All three caves were thoroughly searched for the swimmer and any evidence that may be of interest. A single SCUBA tank full of air was found on a ledge above the high-water line and it appeared the swimmer had stashed more SCUBA gear in the same place which he used to make his underwater escape.

Nicolas James Cabot, tu maldito asesino, the captain quietly whispered to himself as he put in a radio-patched call to his friend United States FBI Agent Marty Goodson. He had ordered his crew to take the sailboat in tow to the small naval facility at Puerto Escondido, a few miles north on the east coast of the Mexican Baja Peninsula.

"Hi, Marty, this is your friend Captain Hugo Chávez."

"How's it going, Hugo? Were you able to find anything on Nick Cabot?"

"Yes, we found something alright. He killed two of my men and then escaped," Captain Chávez noted.

"Oh no, I don't know what to say. I am so sorry, Hugo.

Are you sure it is him; did you get a look at him?"

"No, we were not able to positively identify him, but everything was as you suspected. He was aboard the sailboat Just Dandy with a girlfriend who says she knows nothing about his past. There is some interesting paperwork and other items aboard the sailboat you might like to look over. There was a business card with the name Karter Truman, Yakima County Prosecutor, and a local Mexican phone number written on the back of the card."

"OK, I will be on the next flight to Loreto if that is acceptable to you. We really want to get this rogue cop in custody before he hurts anyone else. The Yakima Field Office can do without me for a few days," Marty stated.

"Good, Marty, just let me know when you arrive, and I will pick you up at the Loreto airport."

"OK, see you soon," Marty replied as they signed off.

1.

BAJA MÉXICO

"Hello, Joe? This is Marty Goodson. How is everything with you?"

"Hi, Marty. I'm doing well. State Farm Insurance Company is keeping me busy."

"Joe, I called you because Nick Cabot has possibly been located down on the Mexican Baja Peninsula. I'm headed there tomorrow, and I thought you might be interested in coming along."

"Yes, I am interested. Do you think you can get me on your flight?"

"Already done, Joe. We will be taking the director's jet, a Grumman Gulfstream II from the Yakima Air Terminal at McAllister Field at 9 tomorrow morning and expect to land at Loreto, Baja Sur by early afternoon."

"That is impressive, Marty. It appears director Hoover is interested in getting Nick Cabot in jail."

"Yes, and Hoover has pulled some strings with the Mexican government to get us the assistance we may need."

"I will need to clear it with my supervisor, but I don't anticipate any problems. See you at the Yakima airport Flight Deck Restaurant at 8AM tomorrow morning."

Joe got approval for time off from his investigative work at

State Farm Insurance and explained the trip to his wife Lydia.

"Joe, we were married not that long ago and now you are leaving for an undetermined length of time to México?" Lydia asked.

"You and I will be living with the possibility Nicolas Cabot could reappear and try again to kill me, unless he is arrested," Joe explained.

"I know but going after him is almost like asking for trouble. I understand what you have to do, and I support you because I love you, but I don't have to like it."

"I don't like it either, Lydia, but once Nicolas Cabot is in custody, we can live our lives in peace. I will be home soon," Joe said as they embraced.

Joe then made a phone call to Jim Sorenson, his former Yakima Police Department foot patrol partner.

"Hi, Jim, this is Joe, how do you like retirement?"

"I am doing well, Joe. My days are filled with so many family activities I can hardly keep up."

"Have you heard anything from the Tunnel Rats?"

"Yes, Squeezy, Sniffer, Snake and Bones are all doing well the last time I talked to them. They asked about you, Lydia and Marty."

"Jim, I called to tell you Nick Cabot has been located down on the Mexican Baja Peninsula. Marty and I will be flying out tomorrow morning for Loreto. Would you like to go? I am sure Marty would welcome you."

"I would love to help you bring in the guy who tried to kill you; if only I was ten years younger. I have hoped that someone would catch up with Cabot, but I am afraid I would be more of a hindrance than a help. Someone should keep an eye out for your raggedy ass. Nick Cabot is a former Army Special Forces soldier with a lot of Vietnam experience, and he is extremely dangerous."

"You have to be smarter than him. Please be careful Joe."

"Yes, I know, thank you, and I promise to be careful."

The next morning over coffee in the Flight Deck Restaurant Joe and Marty discussed plans for travel to México on the Gulfstream II business jet which was parked on the tarmac at McAllister Field.

"Joe, I would like to introduce you to Buck Buchanan, our pilot. Buck is a former Vietnam F-4 Phantom jet fighter pilot with numerous endorsements on his pilots' license, including glider, sea plane, helicopter and high altitude."

"Hi Joe, nice to meet you. He forgot to mention tail-wheel endorsement. It will be nice hanging out with some warriors instead of the director for a change," Buck said with a grin. "I've plotted a course to Loreto, Baja California Sur, México, filed my flight plan and am ready to head for old México whenever you are," Buck stated.

"Here Joe, this is a diplomatic passport for you to use on this assignment. I was able to obtain it in a hurry through the State Department," Marty said as he handed Joe a black newly issued diplomatic passport.

During their walk to the parked business jet, Buck explained some of the aircraft's features.

"She has two Rolls Royce turbofan engines mounted aft that will push her to a speed just shy of the sound barrier. She has a range of over 4000 miles with a ceiling of 45,000 feet. She can carry about 3000 pounds, including passengers with seats for 10 people, if necessary. This aircraft also has a hardened armory which is well stocked for our trip to México," Buck explained.

"What's in the armory?" Joe asked.

"Just about anything you might need. Two China Lake 40 mm grenade launchers with plenty of ammo, five M-16's and ammo, five AK-47's and ammo, five MAC-10 sub machine guns and extra clips of ammo, a case of frag grenades and three Claymore mines. The director knew you would probably be going up against organized drug runners to capture this rogue cop. I assume you are packing your own personal firearms. Diplomatic passports will allow us to carry firearms, including what is in the armory into México without breaking their laws," Buck explained.

"This is Annie Diaz, copilot and Spanish interpreter, and one of the best shots with a .45 pistol anywhere," Buck stated as they entered the cockpit area of the aircraft.

"Hi guys. Marty and Joe, I don't think we've met."

"Nice to meet you, Annie."

"This is Hank Carter and Jack Rosen, FBI SWAT team members. They are coming along to help keep us safe," Buck explained.

"Any relation to Bobby Rosen?" Joe asked.

"He was my brother, killed in the Yakima Convention Center battle," Agent Rosen responded.

"My condolences and thank you for helping us get these affairs resolved," Joe said.

"It is my honor sir and the least I could do for my brother."

"Have you been briefed on our mission?" Marty asked.

"Only that we are going to Loreto México and looking for a rogue cop," Annie responded.

"Annie, Joe and I will fill the three of you in on the details while we're enroute if you can break away from the cockpit for a few minutes," Marty suggested.

"Sounds good. Let's get this show on the road," she responded as she headed back into the cockpit for the preflight check.

"Setting destination coordinates to 25 degrees, 59 minutes and 21 seconds North, and 111 degrees, 20 minutes, 54 seconds West, the Loreto, Baja México, Municipal Airport. We should arrive in just under four hours, depending on the winds," Buck yelled from the cockpit as they were taking off.

"We will be flying south over Oregon, Nevada and Arizona before we come to the Sea of Cortez. I will take us down to an altitude that will allow you to see some of the remote fishing villages on the east coast of the Baja Peninsula before we arrive at Loreto," Buck said as the jet aircraft climbed quickly to thirty thousand feet.

"There are soft drinks and water in the galley refrigerator along with some sandwiches if you get hungry," Annie announced over the intercom.

"Don't flush the toilet in the head while sitting on it. You might get an unexpected thrill. When we are traveling five hundred miles per hour, the vacuum flush can be a bit strong," Buck explained laughing while Marty, Joe, Hank and Jack settled in for the long flight.

"Thanks for the heads-up, pun intended," Joe responded.

The weather was clear with a little tailwind according to Annie. The flight was calm and uneventful and since the aircraft was on autopilot, with Buck keeping an eye on things, Annie was able to make her way back to the cabin and sat down near Marty and Joe.

"I can give you three an outline of what brought us to this point in a couple minutes if you have the time," Marty said.

"Sure Marty, go ahead please," Annie responded.

"It all began with Joe here. He was a young foot patrolman in the downtown area of Yakima City, and he began noticing some suspicious activities taking place on the street and in city and county governments several years ago. I got to know Joe and his partner Reserve Sergeant Jim Sorenson since I worked out of the FBI's Yakima Field Office. With the help of FBI Agents specializing in intelligence and technology, thirty SWAT Officers, including Jack's brother Bobby, four former Vietnam Tunnel Rat soldiers, and thanks to information from a convicted murderer and a grand jury investigation, we were able to get forty-eight federal warrants for officials up to, and including the Yakima County prosecutor, the chief of police, a police captain, the county sheriff, numerous mob soldiers and drug dealers. We are now after the only bad guy that got away, former Yakima Police

5

Narcotics Detective Nicolas James Cabot. Nick slipped away during a gun battle and returned a short time later in an attempt to kill Joe," Marty stated.

"He missed me and now it's my turn to go after him. Instead of referring to him as Nick Cabot I would ask that we just call him Nicky." Joe said with a smile.

"That sounds good to me. We are on our way, Nicky; it is just a matter of time before you are captured and put where you belong," Marty responded.

2.

A BRIEF ENCOUNTER

"We will be entering Mexican airspace in about 3 minutes," Buck announced over the intercom.

"Holy Cow, what is that?" yelled Annie from the cockpit.

Joe and Marty looked through the open cockpit door and out through the windshield of the aircraft at a large, white, cylindrical shaped object, pacing their aircraft about a quarter mile ahead. The object then darted to their starboard side and then quickly moved over to the port side where it remained for about ten minutes.

It must be forty feet long with rounded ends and a tube or something protruding fore and aft at the bottom of the craft, Marty thought to himself.

"Does anyone have a camera?" Joe asked.

"Yes, I do," Annie responded as she grabbed a thirty-five-millimeter Nikon camera from her bag.

She began taking pictures as the strange craft paced the Gulfstream II aircraft at over five hundred miles per hour. The craft then slowly descended towards the Sea of Cortez until it disappeared into the water just southeast of Isla Tortuga, near the village of Santa Rosalia, on the east side of the Baja Peninsula.

"That was incredible! Have any of you ever seen anything

like that before?" Annie asked, while putting her camera back in the bag.

"Yea, it's getting to be routine. I should have mentioned it to you before we left," Buck added.

"You've seen this craft before?" Joe asked.

"Yes, it seems every time we are loaded with weapons, we get checked out by a UFO. They were all over the skies above Vietnam," Buck explained.

"Should we report it to the Federal Aviation Agency?" Annie asked.

"Only if you feel like having to take psychological and polygraph tests and be interrogated for the next month or two. You can also bet your photographs will disappear," Buck responded.

"I wonder where it went?" Joe asked.

"The Sea of Cortez is almost two miles deep in places and if that thing is what I think it is, going down two miles underwater would be no problem for it," Buck concluded.

"I'm just glad we didn't collide with it. It came very close to us," Marty commented.

3.

Loreto Village & Puerto Escondido

The mission at Loreto was established in 1697 by Catholic Jesuit Missionary Juan Maria de Salvatierra, who found a small spring of fresh water at the location. It was the first successful mission on the Baja Peninsula. Today it is connected to the rest of the Baja Peninsula by the new Trans Peninsular Federal Highway 1, which connects with Tijuana City on the northern border with the United States, and travels south all the way to Cabo San Lucas, at the southern tip of the peninsula. An extension of California's Sierra Madre Mountains, called the Sierra de la Giganta, traverses the length of the peninsula separating the Pacific Ocean from the Sea of Cortez. The area has long been known for excellent fishing and as a winter tourist destination for United States and Canadian citizens.

"Time to fasten your seatbelts and say a little prayer we are able to safely land on this dirt runway which is not quite long enough for this beast," Buck announced over the intercom.

The landing was uneventful except for large clouds of dust that kicked up when the jet aircraft landed on the dirt runway and as it taxied to a parking spot at the north end of the unimproved airfield. After the twin jet engines began winding down, a navy gray Chevrolet four-wheel drive Suburban with dark tinted windows drove slowly toward the parked aircraft. Two airport ground support personnel also approached the aircraft and placed chocks under the wheels and assisted with opening the aircraft door. A tall, slim, nicely dressed gentleman in civilian clothing, about thirty-five years old, got out from behind the wheel of the Suburban while two uniformed, armed Mexican Navy police officers got out from the passenger side.

Marty, Joe, Annie, and Buck all climbed down onto the dusty ground.

"Marty, it is good to see you," the gentleman in civilian clothing said.

"Captain Hugo Chávez, my old friend, how are you?" Marty asked as they shook hands.

"I am good, Marty. It looks like you have lost a little weight. Are you taking care of yourself?"

"I've been under a lot of pressure to get this mess cleaned up with the arrest of Nick Cabot. I really appreciate your help, Hugo, and my condolences to you and the families of the men you lost."

"Let me introduce you to the team," Marty continued. "Joe, Annie, Buck this is Captain Hugo Chávez of the Armada de México, the Mexican Navy. We met about ten years ago at the Quantico Virginia FBI Academy where Hugo and I were taking some law enforcement classes. Hugo this is Joe, Annie, and Buck. The two guys in the doorway of the aircraft are Jack and Hank. They will be staying aboard while we are here for security purposes," Marty said as Hank and Jack greeted Hugo with a wave from the airplane's doorway.

"This is Jose Rios and Carlos Silva. They will be guarding your aircraft and the surrounding area while it is parked here at the airport," Hugo responded as he presented the two navy police officers.

"Jack and Hank, if there is anything you need, just let

10

my men know. They have been instructed to provide you with any requests," Captain Hugo Chávez explained.

"Thank you, sir," both Jack and Hank responded.

"Marty, Joe, Annie and Buck, if you like we can go to our small naval facility at Puerto Escondido which is about 20 kilometers south of here," Hugo said as they got into the gray Suburban. During the drive south on Mexican Highway 1 to Puerto Escondido Hugo shared some history and information about the local area.

"Puerto Escondido in Spanish means 'hiding hole' like a place for sailors to hide during a windstorm. Puerto Escondido is a series of bays that provide protection from winds and ocean surges coming from any direction. United States author John Steinbeck dedicated more than one chapter in his book, *The Log from the Sea of Cortez*, published in 1940, to Puerto Escondido. We have a small Navy facility and there is a marina nearby, mostly used by local fishermen. It is an excellent bay, and I am sure you will enjoy the beauty of the area," Hugo explained.

"I have provided you with a cover for your visit to answer any questions the locals may have about your presence, so, officially you are friends of mine now on vacation and will be spending some time sailing and exploring the area at your leisure. You will be living aboard a 63-foot aluminum sailboat named 'Hannah' captained by Kirk Christian. We have leased the boat and services of the skipper for as long as it takes to complete your mission. Captain Kirk has taken an oath of confidentiality and will take you on the boat wherever you need to go," Hugo continued.

"You will also have the complete backing of the Mexican Navy and our assets in your mission. Let us now get you settled in your new domicile," Hugo continued as they stopped at the civilian dock at Puerto Escondido.

Tied at the end of the dock was the 63-foot Deerfoot aluminum cutter sailboat called "Hannah". Packing their gear out to the end of the dock, they were greeted by skipper Kirk Christian.

"This is your crew for the time being. Joe, Marty, Annie, and Buck," Hugo explained.

"Welcome folks, please come aboard and make yourselves at home," Captain Kirk replied.

4.

SAILING VESSEL HANNAH

"SV Hannah has two staterooms with two bunk beds in each, plus the captain's master suite. Annie, you get one stateroom to yourself, and Marty and Joe can share the third stateroom. Buck, you can take the quarter berth on the starboard side of the salon. Each stateroom has its own head and shower and if any of you would like to take a bath instead of a shower just let me know and you can use the bathtub in the captain's suite. The galley is fully stocked, but is in need of a chef, so if any of you want to volunteer for that task, feel free to do so," Captain Kirk stated.

"I would ask you to check the soles of your footwear to be sure they are not making marks on the decks and please be aware of your usage of electric power from the boat's batteries. I understand you have a mission and I have great respect for you law officers. I will help you any way I can. We are supposed to be on vacation so let us break out some soft drinks and some excellent Mexican beer while Captain Hugo gives us a briefing," Kirk suggested.

"Thanks, Kirk. Yes, let me bring you up to speed on our contact with Nicolas James Cabot or 'Nicky' as we call him. This man killed two of my young sailors in a most brutal fashion. Sailors Luis Marquez and Jose Salinas, both family men with wives, children and large extended families, lost their lives to your murdering former police officer. If it was up to us, we would have very specific plans for this *hombre*, but since he is one of yours, we will assist you to bring him to your justice," Hugo began.

"We believe, through his work as a narcotics detective Nicky was able to make a number of contacts here in México with narco traffickers. Since we now know Nicky was working with your local underworld and has a warrant for his arrest, we believe he made preparations with his Mexican narco-contacts some time ago to disappear among them if and when it became necessary. We acted on your tip, Marty, that Nicky may be living aboard Sailing Vessel Just Dandy with a Mexican girlfriend. We found SV Just Dandy anchored in a remote bay not far from here and when we approached, Nicky went overboard and swam to a nearby sea cave. I sent divers Luis and Jose to locate him in the cave and take him into custody. Luis was stabbed 11 times and died in the water of his wounds while Jose was strangled with a rope and hung-up dead, like a trophy, in the cave. We believe Nicky made preparations for his escape ahead of time by stashing SCUBA gear and what sailors call a 'ditch bag' in the caves. He got away from us by swimming underwater with SCUBA gear, underneath and past our vessel, with a battery powered swimmer delivery vehicle or SDV," Hugo continued.

"We think he got out of the water on the outside of the bay where he had a *panga* available to him. From there we do not know where he went. We do believe, however, he is still on or near the Sea of Cortez and possibly not far from us now. He has had extensive training as a United States Army Ranger and is easily capable of surviving in the wilds of the Baja Peninsula or in the Sonoran Desert on the Mexican mainland," Hugo stated.

"What is a *panga*?" Buck asked.

"A *panga* is an open fishing skiff powered by outboard motors and is common in México and Central American countries. Viewed from the side, the shape of the bow resembles a knife called a *panga* or machete," Hugo explained.

"Where can we start looking for Nicky?" Marty asked.

"I have some confidential informants working on locating Nicky and expect they will get back to me in a few days. Meanwhile, I suggest you get yourselves settled here on Hannah. Captain Kirk wants to do some sailing to help you understand and perform the duties of a sailing crew. This will give you some time to turn yourselves into Hannah's crew," Hugo noted with a smile.

"Aye, aye, clear the decks!" Buck responded.

Later Captain Kirk patiently explained the rigging and the duties of the sailing crew while Hannah was tied to the slip at Puerto Escondido. He then started the diesel motor, explained how the exhaust needs to be checked for water emerging that cools the motor, and ordered the dock lines to be cast off. SV Hannah motored quietly through the inner passage to the outer bay and onto the Sea of Cortez for a shakedown cruise.

When Hannah's nose was pointed north into the wind, Captain Kirk ordered, "take to the halyard and raise the main sail!" Then, "heave the jib halyards."

As the two foresails were deployed, Captain Kirk sailed south with a ten-knot breeze coming out of the northwest, past Isla Dazante and Honeymoon Bay. Almost immediately, as the boat was moving silently through the water and while the crew relaxed from their duties, splashing was heard coming from near the bow of the sailboat.

"It's a pod of dolphins!" Annie yelled. "They are swimming alongside us. I'm going to get my camera," she said as she headed toward the companionway to her cabin.

Hannah sailed easily south for the next couple of hours.

"I thought you might like to take a look at the bay and

village at Agua Verde," Captain Kirk said. "We should arrive there in an hour or so."

Isla Monscratte came into view and Bahia Agua Verde was located southwest, just a few more miles. As they later rounded the point entering the bay at Agua Verde, everyone was tense knowing this was the last place Nicky was seen and where two young Mexican sailors were brutally killed.

"I can make out the name of the sailboat off our port bow," Marty stated while looking through field glasses. "It's SV Kylahi. She is about a forty-foot sloop, and I don't see anyone aboard," Marty continued. "The other one is SV Cleo II, a little shorter, and neither has a dinghy tied to them so my guess is they are ashore. Let me see if I can reach Hugo at the Navy base in Puerto Escondido by radio. He may be able to give us more information about these sail-boats and their skippers," Marty said as he headed down the companionway to the radio at the chart table.

"Let's drop anchor between them," Captain Kirk stated as he moved the boat in position.

After engaging the windlass and dropping the 55-pound Rocna anchor in 30 feet of water and deploying one hundred fifty feet of chain, Captain Kirk put the diesel motor in reverse and slowly tightened up on the chain, making sure the anchor dug deep into the sandy bottom. A short while later Marty returned to the cockpit from below.

"According to Captain Hugo, SV Kylahi is owned by a Canadian politician-businessman and appears to be clean. SV Cleo II is owned by a French banker from the San Francisco area, and there does not appear to be any problems with this boat or its owner," Marty explained.

"It is almost suppertime, and it will be dark soon. Let's keep an eye on things around here while we prepare a meal, then relax and examine the area closer tomorrow morning," Marty suggested.

"That sounds good," Joe said while he continued to look

the other sailboats over closely with field glasses.

"You know, Marty, Hugo lost his men to an army special forces tactic. One stages the area you are in ahead of time for a confrontation and prepares for a quick escape if necessary. The thing that infuriates me about Nicky is that part of his plan was to lure his enemy to a position of vulnerability, prior to the kill. After the kill, he celebrated by hanging his victim up for all to see. The two young men and their families meant nothing to Nicky. He has skills only taught to special forces soldiers. My guess is the Vietnam War has not ended for him and we are now his enemy," Joe reasoned.

"I think you may be right. If you are right, Nicky will probably try to lure us into a trap to kill us," Marty responded.

"We need someone here that knows how Nicky thinks," Joe suggested.

"One of the tunnel rats was in Army Special Forces if I remember correctly. Was it Snake?" Marty asked.

"Yes Marty, I think you're right. Snake was special forces and I know he would be here in a heartbeat if he knew we could use his help."

"He worries me a little though Joe. It seems he could come unhinged unexpectedly and I would not want that to happen here in México."

"I think I could keep a close eye on him in the event things begin to happen. He's the help we need."

"OK, Joe, I will call my secretary the next time we get near a telephone and ask her if she will call him and get him set up to fly into Cabo on a commercial airline where we could pick him up, or we could send Buck to go get him. Snake would probably like that. I wonder what the director would think of that?" Marty asked.

"The sacrifices Snake has given to our country qualifies him more than almost anyone else I can think of," Joe said.

"You are right again Joe. But if I get my hide nailed to the wall I'm going to say, 'Joe made me do it,'" Marty responded while laughing.

"Come and get it," Buck yelled from the galley.

Everyone lined up for a plate of spaghetti with parmesan cheese and a glass of a Mexican cabernet wine. Marty, Joe and Annie took their plates up to the cockpit while Kirk and Buck ate in the salon at the large table.

Joe prayed, "Bless this food, Lord, and watch over your servants in the work we do. Lead us and guide us to achieve your glory, in Jesus' name we pray."

"Amen," Marty and Annie responded.

The sun was setting in the west behind the Sierra Gianta mountains and the last rays lit up the tall, majestic, rocky point at the entrance to the bay. Water in the bay was disturbed in some areas as bait fish schooled and jumped out of the water attempting to avoid the larger fish chasing them. "Whoosh, whoosh," came the sound across the water as a pod of dolphins moved toward SV Hannah.

"Look, two dolphins have broken away from the pack and are headed this way. Let's see what they are up to," Joe said as he put his fork down.

Two larger dolphins came toward SV Hanna's starboard side, swam around her stern and back toward the pod on Hannah's port side.

"It looks like those two dolphins that broke away are herding the school of fish," Marty observed.

"Yes, and now they've met and are slapping the water with their tails to stun the baitfish. What an interesting place!" Annie exclaimed.

The next morning after breakfast Joe, Marty, Annie and Buck lowered SV Hannah's tender, a twelve-foot inflatable dinghy with a 25 horsepower Mercury outboard motor, from where she hung on davits at the stern of the sailboat. Leaving Captain Kirk aboard Hannah, they took a slow tour of the bay in the dinghy, especially looking over the sea caves where the two Mexican sailors died. They motored slowly past a goat farm tucked away in the southwest corner of the bay.

"Those goats were what was making the sound of tinkling bells we could hear last night," Annie remarked.

They landed in the center of the beach and pulled the dinghy up on the sand, so it would not float away, and went for a walk. They walked toward a small structure, which appeared to be temporary, on the upper part of the beach and in approaching they realized it was a small, rustic beach restaurant.

"I wonder if they have cold beer," Joe was thinking out loud as a Mexican woman in her 40's motioned them to take a seat.

The floor was sand, the table and chairs were wooden fold-up camping type furniture. The walls and roof were plywood and there was a section in the rear where the woman had a griddle and an oven along with a refrigerator.

"*Buenos Días. Bienvenidos a el restaurante Leona,*" the lady greeted.

Annie, fluent in Spanish, had a conversation with her and said, "This is Leona and back behind there is her husband, Enrique. Leona runs this little restaurant and Enrique is a fisherman," Annie explained.

"Please sit down," Leona said as she gave Annie a hand-written menu.

"We might as well, since it is almost lunch time," Buck said.

"*Camarones, pescado, pulpo, mariscos frescos,* shrimp, fish, octopus, fresh seafood," Annie read from the menu.

While Leona was preparing their orders, Annie was quietly speaking Spanish with Enrique.

"Who ordered the octopus?" Buck asked, and after a pause stated, "What! No one ordered the octopus; we are a bunch of wimps."

"Why didn't you order octopus?" Marty asked.

"I guess 'cause I'm a wimp too," Buck said laughing.

After finishing lunch, they continued their walk around

the bay and since the tide was out, they were able to get a look into the sea caves at the north end of the bay. They approached the mouth of the first cave and looked into it but did not enter because sea water still covered the floor of the cave to a depth of about three feet. As they stood at the entrance looking deep into the dark depths, a cold breeze blew across the entrance causing a low moaning sound to echo into the cave as the gust of wind swept past them.

"Burrr, this is one spooky place," Annie declared as they all stepped back.

"It feels like another place I've been to in Yakima. Evil spirits seem to like hanging out in underground places." Joe said as they turned around and began walking back to their dinghy.

Back at SV Hannah, Annie couldn't wait to tell the team what she had learned from her conversation with Enrique.

"I spoke to Enrique in Spanish while Leona was preparing lunch and I learned quite a bit," Annie stated. "I told Enrique I was looking for my old boyfriend named 'Nicky' and I heard he was hanging around Agua Verde."

"What did he say?" Marty asked.

"He said he was the Pope, and he would forgive me for lying to him. He wanted to know if we were FBI or CIA, so I asked him if he could keep a secret from his family and friends. He said he would, and he wanted me to know that he may be a simple fisherman, but he was not stupid. He said he can read and gets week old newspapers sometimes, and he has a portable radio with an antenna that goes to the top of a tree. He then asked me what I wanted to know about the man they know as Nicolas?"

"Everything, I told him."

"He started off by telling me Nicolas is evil, one can see it in his eyes. He smiles at you, but his eyes are filled with evil. Enrique told me about an encounter Nicolas had with a nun who teaches at the village school. Evidently the nun was at the village market, and she unexpectedly came face to face with Nicolas. The nun tells people his head was like that of a dragon the moment she first saw him and as she continued to look at him, his face changed back to that of a man. The nun told them Nicolas was evil and they should be very careful around him and constantly carry their rosaries. Enrique said that Nicolas avoided the nun. He would turn around and walk away when he saw her approaching. Nicolas bought a *panga* from Enrique's friend and paid double what it was worth in Mexican pesos. Enrique said Nicolas always carries a large amount of cash and a dagger. The girlfriend is actually the owner of the sailboat Just Dandy that the Mexican Navy towed away. Her name is Lola Flores and Enrique describes her as a moll (*companera de los desperados*) for the bad guys from the mainland that hang around Agua Verde. The bad guys come from the Guadalajara cartel and are probably on the run from police or hit men on the Mexican mainland, according to Enrique. Enrique says he wants them to stay away from his village, and he is afraid of them. Enrique does not want us here either, but he understands we are the good guys. He agreed to help us, but he does not want to put his village in danger. He wants us to make sure his people are safe from harm. I assured him we would do everything we could, and he is right, those men are bad, and anything could happen, but we would try to keep his village safe. About that time lunch was ready so our conversation ended," Annie stated.

"Let's post a watch tonight since we are so obviously not tourists. I will take the first watch until 3AM," Marty volunteered.

"I will take the second watch Marty."

"Thanks, Joe, the rest of you sleep well. Tomorrow we head back to the Puerto Escondido Navy facility and meet up with Hugo," Marty added.

"Good work, Annie, way to go with Enrique," Joe exclaimed.

"Annie, maybe we should see if Enrique will go with us tomorrow, to see what else he might tell us?" Joe asked.

"I could run in on the dinghy before the restaurant closes this afternoon and see if he would go with us for a couple days."

"That is a good idea, Annie. I agree, go ahead and see what he says," Marty responded.

It was over a mile to the beach, and it was getting dark when Annie returned. She had to look for SV Hannah's anchor light at the top of the mast. Captain Kirk also turned on the sailboat's running lights for Annie.

When she climbed aboard, she said, "He will be at the beach at 6 AM waiting for the dinghy to pick him up."

"Good job, Annie, see all of you at 5 AM for breakfast since I will be the chef," Buck said with a smile.

The next morning after breakfast, and as soon as Enrique arrived aboard, Captain Kirk started the diesel motor. After it warmed up, they motored out onto the Sea of Cortez. Turning the boat into a west breeze, Captain Kirk called for the sails to be raised and then turned north and sailed pleasantly on a beam-reach. About five hours later, when SV Hannah was about to fetch the entrance to Puerto Escondido, Captain Kirk turned the boat to luff the sails. He called for the head sails to be rolled up, the mainsail brought down and furled, while he started the diesel motor and then slowly entered the harbor at Puerto Escondido.

Captain Hugo greeted them, took a line and tied SV Hannah to a cleat on the marina dock.

"We have some new information, Hugo. I would like you to meet Enrique Garcia from Agua Verde," Marty announced.

"*Mucho gusto*," they greeted each other as they shook hands.

"I will explain more later," Marty continued as they walked down the dock to the Navy building.

"Did you learn how to be good sailors?" Hugo asked.

"It is a little different than flying an airplane," Buck responded.

Hugo said, "I have prepared the conference room for us to discuss the events and to plan our tactics. Staff will keep the doors closed and the room secure so that all the information we discuss will remain private."

5.

TARGET – NICOLAS JAMES CABOT

" I have asked that our supper be provided for us here so we can use all the time we need to proceed. There is a restroom with a shower through that door and several cots in the corner for those who pulled a night watch and want to take a nap," Hugo explained.

"OK, let's see what information and questions we have up to this point. Enrique, please feel free to be included and, Annie, if you would interpret for him what is being said, we would appreciate it," Marty stated.

"Prosecutor Karter Truman's business card with the local phone number is interesting. Karter always made his sevens with a horizontal line through the number just like what is written on the back of this business card. I would bet that Karter wrote this number down before he died in the car accident in Yakima some time ago," Joe asserted.

"The question still remains; how did that card get down here in México and on SV Just Dandy?" Annie asked.

"There's something else," Joe continued. "The phone number has no country code or area code. Just the local number. It may mean something, but I'm not sure what," Joe said while Annie interpreted for Enrique.

"The number comes back to a cartel member who lives

up in the mountains and keeps an airplane at the Loreto Airport. His name is Pablo Escobar. He is rumored to be a Columbian drug kingpin and he does not spend much time on the Mexican Baja. His plane is at the airport now so he may also be here. The Mexican Navy has a dossier worked up on him and since the phone number led us to his name, I brought a copy of the dossier for the team to look over." Hugo added.

"As you can see, the cabin is in the mountains near the village of San Javier which is about 25 miles west of Loreto."

"Marty, if Buck has been authorized to go get Snake in the jet aircraft and bring him here, maybe he can do a fly-over of this cabin and get some photos of it from the plane's belly camera," Joe suggested.

"That's an excellent idea, Joe. Let me call my secretary and find out if Snake has agreed to help us, and if so, some photos would be a big help," Marty agreed.

"All you need to do is give me the coordinates of the cabin and I will take some nice photos for you," Buck offered.

A short while later Marty returned to the room to advise, "Buck, Snake has agreed to help us and is ready to go anytime you can pick him up."

"OK, if you give me Snake's phone number, I will call him and let him know when I will arrive. Let me also write down the coordinates for that cabin," Buck said as he looked through the Mexican Navy dossier on Pablo Escobar.

"We need to debrief Enrique and get him back to his family as soon as possible. Why don't we do that now?" Joe asked as Annie interpreted for Enrique.

"How can we find Lola Flores? I'm sure she could give us some helpful information on Nicky, if we could trust her."

"Her word is good. She is very angry with Nicky and would like to see him do some time in jail," Annie interpreted for Enrique.

Enrique also explained, through Annie, that Lola's family

lives at Agua Verde, and they are ashamed and incredibly sad over their daughter's behavior running with bad men. She occasionally returns to Agua Verde in her sailboat with friends and sometimes with her boyfriend. She always has money and tries to give some to family and friends but most of the village stays away from her. When she was with Nicky at the market a couple weeks ago, she had a black eye, her cheek was swollen and when one of her friends asked her what happened she said Nicky hit her," Annie interpreted for Enrique.

"Ask Enrique if he could find Lola and bring her to us without the bad guys finding out?" Joe suggested.

"Sometimes she comes to Puerto Escondido with her uncle, who is a fisherman. Enrique says if he hears she is coming this way he will send word to me."

"Please explain to Enrique, we will take him back to his family at Agua Verde in a *panga* soon. Ask him to keep silent about us and our plans," Joe said to Annie.

"He agrees," Annie responded.

"I have an unmarked *panga* with a 100 hp outboard that can quickly take Enrique back to Agua Verde before dark if you want to keep his contact with the navy confidential. I will have one of my sailors in civilian clothes return him now to Agua Verde if you wish," Hugo advised.

"Yes, that would be a big help. Thank you, Hugo. Thank you very much Enrique for your help. Is there anything we can do for you before you leave?" Marty asked.

"Yes, he could use some new batteries for his portable radio," Annie responded.

"Here is a box of D cell batteries for Enrique."

"*Gracias, muchas gracias*," Enrique responded to Hugo as he left the room with a young Mexican sailor.

The next day was spent looking over maps and naval charts of the sea and mountains from Agua Verde to Loreto and especially the mountainous area around San Javier by

Joe, Marty, Annie and Hugo. In the early afternoon a *panga* came unannounced into the marina at Puerto Escondido with Enrique at the tiller and a young Mexican woman sitting in the bow.

"*Esta es Lola Flores*," Enrique said as he approached Joe on the dock.

"Yes, who are you?" Lola asked in slightly broken English.

"I am Joe. Nice to meet you. I've heard a lot about you," Joe responded.

"Have you heard I want to kill that *maldito* Nicky?" Lola asked.

"Why would you want to do that?" Joe asked.

"Because he is a *pendejo*."

"How do we know we can trust you?"

"You don't. But you know we both want the same thing. Nicky in jail *verdad?*"

"Yes, true. Let's go someplace where we can get a cold drink and relax, and you can tell me all about Nicky," Joe suggested as they headed down the dock."

"*Regreso a mi casa,*" Enrique stated as he pushed his *panga* off and started the outboard motor.

"He is going back home. *Gracias,*" Lola said as she waved to Enrique.

Hugo, Buck, and Snake had arrived from the Loreto airport and were present in the navy conference room along with Annie and Marty when Joe and Lola entered the room.

"I would like to introduce to you Lola Flores. Lola is another victim of Nicky's violence, and she is here to help us get Nicky in custody. I will let you each introduce yourselves to Lola," Joe informed everyone.

"I should also introduce Snake to those who do not know him," Marty said. "Snake prefers to be called by his nickname which he earned as a warrior fighting in Vietnam's underground tunnels. He belongs to an exclusive group of slightly built men called Tunnel Rats who routinely entered the enemy's tunnels armed only with a pistol, a flashlight and a knife, on search and destroy missions. Snake was also a United States Army Ranger as was Nicky. Snake has agreed to help us understand Nicky's capabilities and plan his capture. Please feel free to also introduce yourselves to Snake," Marty added. After a few minutes of introductions, chatting and socializing Marty called for everyone's attention.

"I would like Snake to explain to us the training and experiences of an Army Ranger, like what he and Nick Cabot went through. Lola will then most likely want to tell us the latest information she has on Nicolas Cabot or Nicky, as we call him. First, please help us understand Nicky's capabilities, Snake."

"Thank you, Sir. Nicky and I were members of the United States 75th Army Ranger Regiment at Fort Benning, Georgia. Nicky completed Ranger School a couple of years after me. I met him once, and later heard he was doing incredible things in Vietnam. The training we received and the activities we were trained to conduct were, and still are, classified as restricted.

Please keep the information I am about to share with you to yourselves in the interest of national security. Besides learning how to operate almost every weapon devised by man, we were instructed on how to defeat an enemy, not only physically but also emotionally and spiritually. I will not go into the details, but we were given information on how to destabilize and bring down foreign governments and other organizations. We learned how to turn aggression and defensive actions on our part into offensive tricks that confused and disoriented our enemies. These skills were instructed and practiced until we were perfect in achieving devastating results. We learned how to lure the enemy, that was searching for us, to a position of disadvantage to kill him. From what I have heard about the encounter at Agua Verde, that is exactly what Nicky did to the Mexican sailors.

I caution you to remember how dangerous this man is while you are attempting to arrest him. I would be surprised if we are able to find Nicky in such a compromising position where he would have to surrender. I expect if we can corner Nicky, he would probably take his own life instead of going to jail. I am honored to be part of this team and I will help in any way I can," Snake concluded.

"Lola has had the most recent contact with Nicky. Would you be willing to answer some questions from the team, Lola?" Marty asked.

"Sure, what do you want to know?"

"Where do you think he is now?" Joe asked.

"I think he is with Pablo at his ranch in the mountains right now."

"Tell us everything you know about Pablo, Nicky and Pablo's ranch," Joe asked.

"OK, Pablo is from Columbia, and he speaks Spanish with a Columbian accent. Pablo is *muy rico*, he has an airplane, a large yacht, and the ranch in the mountains. He has another house in Columbia and he is nice to me. He is friends with Nicky too, and they have known each other for years. The ranch in the mountains near San Javier is very modern with the latest in kitchen appliances, TV's and an alarm system. It has a tall fence that goes all the way around the property, and he has guards with guns for protection," Lola explained.

"What do they do at the ranch during an average day?" Joe asked.

"They get up about 9 AM and have breakfast made for them by the cook. Then they may go riding horses or motorcycles on the trails around the ranch. They go swimming in the pool or watch movies on the TV. Sometimes they get bored and call for women friends to join them at the ranch and sometimes they go to La Paz. They don't go to Loreto because everyone in Loreto knows them. I met Pablo at a bar on the *malecón,* or promenade, in La Paz called The Tailhunter Bar. Pablo and Nicky like the Tailhunter because Nicky likes the Seattle Seahawks football team, and they can watch the Seahawks on the TV there."

"Where do they find women friends and how do they travel to and from the ranch?" Joe asked while the rest of the team listened intently.

"Pablo sometimes has his pilot fly him in the *helicóptero* or they take two black Chevy Suburbans. Pablo has friends on the Baja, and he has phone numbers of the women, or he meets them in a bar. Pablo introduced me to Nicky," Lola explained.

"Is there anything else about Nicky, Pablo and the ranch you can tell us that might be important?" Joe asked.

"Yes, well maybe you should know about the rattlesnakes," Lola responded.

"Please tell us about the rattlesnakes," Snake said with a piercing look in his eyes.

"Pablo likes snakes, and he keeps dozens of them at the ranch in cages like they are his pets. He also has a large open pit area with a pond and landscaped with rocks and cactus just for his snakes so they can feel at home. One time he got mad at a guard and made the guard crawl on his hands and knees across the pit in the dark. The man got bit by several snakes and died the next day. You don't want to make Pablo angry."

"Lola, we appreciate your help, and we hope to get Nicky in custody so he can't hurt anyone else. For your safety I think it would be best if you stayed here with us at the naval facility, until we finish our work. We would not want you to have to crawl through the snake pit after dark, would we?" Marty asked with a smile.

"Yes, I agree to stay here if you have room for me."

"I will show you to your room now if you will follow me," Hugo said.

"Thank you, Lola. Thank you," the team said in unison

as Lola left the room with Captain Hugo.

"That was interesting. Buck, do you have some photos of the ranch Lola described. I was under the impression it was just a small cabin, but it sounds more like a mansion," Marty surmised.

"Yes, I did a high-altitude fly-over and took some photos and then a while later I did a lower altitude pass. Here are the results," Buck said as he laid several photos out on the table.

"That is no cabin, it looks more like a high-class compound surrounded by a fence and in the middle of a cactus and bushy desert mountain landscape," Joe observed as they all looked at the photographs.

"It looks almost impenetrable," Annie remarked.

"Yes, unless we can get someone inside to open the gates," Snake added.

"Let's consider this information tonight and get together here at 9 AM and see if we can come up with a plan to complete this mission," Marty suggested as the team broke up for the evening.

"Marty, we are having a naval base all-staff meeting in the training room in a few minutes and I would like to invite you and your team to attend," Hugo stated.

"Yes, of course. I will pass the word to my team," Marty responded.

Many started gathering in and around the outside of the training room a few minutes before 7 PM. About fifteen young *marineros* dressed in fatigues chatted amongst themselves in Spanish. There were five female *marineras* in the group wearing the same uniforms. The insignia on the uniform of one female *marinera* indicated she was a *Teniente de Corbeta* or a Lieutenant of a Corvette Class vessel. She was tall and slim with long black hair. Her eyes were like large dark pools of liquid that sparkled with intelligence and passion. Her eyelashes were long and beautiful. She moved in a stately manner and occasionally looked quickly around the room at the newcomers and especially at Snake.

"*¡Atención! Por favor vengan a orden,*" came the command as the group stood at attention.

Captain Hugo Chávez entered the room and ordered everyone at ease and to please take their seats. He began speaking in Spanish to the group while FBI Agent and co-pilot Annie Diaz translated quietly.

"Hugo welcomes his sailors to the meeting and says he has some important information to give them. He asks of his sailors to keep what he is about to tell them to themselves, to not even tell their spouses, friends or family members. They are standing now to raise their right hands and give an oath of secrecy," Annie explained.

After giving the oath, the tall female Lieutenant kept glancing at Snake and this time, he noticed her.

Annie continued translating what Captain Hugo was telling the sailors. "He is explaining that a highly trained soldier and former police detective from the United States has turned to crime and is working with a drug cartel in this area. The huge criminal case was exposed by a police foot patrolman faithfully doing his duty. All of the organized criminals in the case have been arrested except for the for-mer police detective. This is the same man who killed your fellow sailors Jose Salinas and Luis Marquez," Annie said, translating Captain Hugo's words.

"These visitors from the United States are very sorry one of their own went bad and killed our friends and fellow sailors. This bad man needs to be brought to justice and these law enforcement people from the United States are here asking for our help in apprehending this killer," Annie interpreted.

A long, respectful applause followed Captain Hugo's words. He then asked if Marty wanted to say anything.

"Yes, thank you, Captain. Annie, if you would kindly translate for me, I would appreciate it," Marty began. "First, I want to express my condolences for the loss of your two sailors and friends, Jose Salinas and Luis Marquez. I bear some responsibility in their loss because I asked your captain, and my friend, to arrest this killer for us. I knew he was dangerous, but I did not realize he had so many deadly skills. When I return to the United States, I will submit a formal request that the names Jose Salinas and Luis Marquez be added to our National Law Enforcement Wall of Honor. Your fellow sailors died serving a request from the people of the United States and I intend to see that their names are also remembered by the citizens of my country, out of our sincere gratitude," Marty announced.

The entire group rose to their feet and applauded Marty's words.

"Please keep our presence to yourselves and remember us and our efforts in your prayers," Marty concluded as the meeting adjourned.

Snake and the Lieutenant were trying to break through the language barrier attempting to communicate with each other.

"I like dangerous men," Joe heard Lieutenant Veronica say to Snake as he walked past them.

At breakfast the next morning discussions began on forming a plan to find and capture Nicolas James Cabot, also known as Nicky.

"I think Lola could lure him out of hiding if it is conducted properly," Annie suggested. "She could let it be known that she is with child and needs to talk to Nicky about it."

After a pause, Snake said, "I think it would be best if we cornered Nicky and Pablo Escobar at their mansion and take them down there. We could take the place apart without fear of collateral damage."

"I think we should check the Seattle Seahawks football team schedule and stake out The Tailhunter Bar in La Paz on game day," Buck suggested.

"I think they are all good ideas, and we should consider all three. One of those plans is bound to work," Joe advised.

"There is just one thing we need to remember," Snake cautioned. "Nicky lured those young Mexican sailors in order to kill them for sport. He didn't need to engage them; he could have escaped without confronting them. He likes killing. He enjoys it. He will lure us just like he did the young Mexican sailors. He is a man with expert skills to kill, and he is without honor. We need to be extremely cautious and outsmart him."

6.

Preliminary Plans

"Let's take this one step at a time. Snake, go first," Marty requested.

"I can stake out the ranch by spending time in the bush near the gate to the ranch and see who comes and goes. If I remember right, there are night vision goggles and long-lens surveillance scopes in the FBI airplane's armory. I can get there easily if I can use one of the 250 Yamaha dirt bikes on the aircraft," Snake proposed.

"Yes and grab one of the marine band hand-held scrambler radios to keep in touch with the rest of the team," Buck agreed.

"Each one of us should have a hand-held radio. I will go with Snake and get what we need. Make sure the scrambled switch is in the on position and let's communicate on channel twenty-two," Buck suggested.

"OK, what about Lola, will she cooperate?" Joe asked.

"I just spoke to her in her room. Yes, she agreed to put out the story that she is pregnant and is looking for Nicky. She is apprehensive about what could happen if Nicky finds out the truth that she has been helping the authorities. I can stay close with her and pose as her friend to protect her and hang out with her to see what happens," Annie asserted.

"I will release her sailboat to her so she can use it to see if Nicky contacts her," Captain Hugo advised.

"The third plan sounds like the best duty," Marty said with a grin. "Buck will go to La Paz posing as a tourist staying at La Perla Hotel and hanging out at the Tailhunter Bar watching Seattle Seahawks football and waiting for Nicky to show up."

"Maybe I should help Buck with this task since I speak a little Spanish," Joe said with a smile.

"Snake should have a backup and somebody to relieve him, so I will suit up in my jungle fatigues," Marty added.

"If anybody spots Nicky, the rest of us have to be ready to move on him in a moment's notice. Let's meet here after lunch to iron out the details," Marty suggested.

"I'm going for lunch at Lieutenant Veronica's apartment. She is going to teach me how to make tamales. See ya later," Snake said, grinning.

Later that afternoon the team got together to discuss the three-pronged plan to locate Nicky. Snake was not present.

"Does anybody know where Snake might be?" Joe asked.

"He is learning to make tamales. I can go get him. He must have lost track of time," Buck responded.

Ten minutes later Buck returned with Snake. The thought of scruffy fifty some year-old Snake together with stately tall brunette Lieutenant Veronica evoked thoughts of odd couples.

"I thought she wanted to show me how to make tamales," Snake said.

"Who's that?" Annie asked.

"Lieutenant Veronica wanted to show me how to make tamales at her apartment. But I must have misunderstood because of the language barrier," Snake explained.

"She then grabbed me and made some sort of reference to a tamale, and I didn't know what to do," Snake said as the team began to snicker.

"What did she say?" Joe asked.

"All she could say was, 'I like dangerous men,'" Snake replied as the team broke out in laughter.

"Buck got weapons and portable radios for us so make sure you have what you need and don't forget your diplomatic passports. Let's all of us check in twice every twenty-four hours. Is ten hundred and twenty-two hundred hours OK? Let's run these missions for no more than a week, is that agreed?" Marty asked.

"Yes," all agreed.

"I will be here waiting for your call to help get this *asesino* Nicky in custody," Hugo said.

Marty and Snake rode away on their motorcycles carrying large backpacks, while Joe and Buck got a ride to the airport where they rented a car so they could drive to La Paz.

Annie and Lola checked the equipment on SV Just Dandy. Annie unfurled the jib and raised the mainsail, moving Just Dandy southbound, running downwind with the sails in a wing-on-wing configuration. They were headed first to Agua Verde in search of Nicky, father of Lola's imaginary unborn child.

Lieutenant Veronica waved at Snake and Marty as they rode by her apartment. Snake blew her a kiss.

Captain Kirk sailed SV Hannah south to a remote bay between Agua Verde and La Paz City, called San Evaristo, and waited for instructions.

FBI SWAT Agents Hank Carter and Jack Rosen continued to guard the Grumman Gulfstream II aircraft parked at the Loreto Airport.

7.

Pablo's Compound

The twenty-mile ride was a daunting trip up into the mountains to the old mission village of San Javier. The route took the riders across two small streams and up a winding narrow dirt road through the mountains until it broke out onto a large plateau. The village of San Javier was located at the far west end of the high desert plain. The old mission church sat in the center of the village where children in uniforms, dismissed from Catholic school, were walking home as Snake and Marty arrived. Motorcycles and dune buggies were not uncommon in San Javier since the Baja 1000 race from Tijuana to Cabo San Lucas had begun a few years prior.

"I could sure stand to stretch my legs," Marty said as he climbed off the motorcycle.

"How about a beer and a taco at that little restaurant?" Snake asked.

"Sounds good to me," Marty responded.

A middle-aged woman wearing a faded print dress and an apron appeared at the table.

"*¿Que queres?*" she asked looking at Marty.

"What does she want?" Marty asked Snake.

"She wants to know what you want," Snake replied.

"A beer and a taco," Marty replied, looking at Snake.

"*¿Que?*" the woman responded, looking at Marty.

"*Cerveza y taco, por favor Señora*," Snake stated in Spanish.

"*¿Para los dos?*" the woman asked.

"*Si, por favor*," Snake replied.

"Thanks, Snake, what is the plan after lunch?" Marty asked.

"I think we should turn around and head back to Loreto since the road ends here. It should almost be dark when we get to the turnoff to Pablo Escobar's mansion. We can hide the bikes and walk into the property until we get to the security gate manned by armed guards. I would like to hide out in the bush while watching the activity coming and going for a while. We can climb the hill above the mansion at night and watch from a hidden location using our spotting scope. Would you recognize Nicky if you saw him through the scope?" Snake asked.

"Yes, I think so, unless he has changed his appearance."

After lunch Marty and Snake rode east, back in the direction from which they came, until they reached the unmarked dirt roadway to Escobar's mansion. The peaks of the Sierra Giantas enveloped the high valley in an early twilight shade as the sun dropped below the tops of the mountains. Looking at the scruffy driveway entrance, one could hardly imagine the opulent mansion at the end of the dirt trail, which was only wide enough for one vehicle.

"Let's find a place to ditch these bikes," Snake said.

They rode off into the desert, past several tall Cardon cacti into a small gully where they laid the motorcycles down and out of sight from the dirt road. They then took some brush and drug it along the ground, erasing the motorcycle tracks.

"If we hear somebody approaching, duck and hide off the trail until they pass," Snake suggested as they began walking up the driveway to the mansion, taking care to leave as few footprints as possible in the dust.

Aerial photographs taken by Buck from the jet aircraft earlier indicated the security checkpoint for the mansion was up the driveway about a mile. Just before approaching the guard shack and checkpoint, Marty and Snake left the driveway and walked out into the surrounding desert past Palo Verde bushes, Cardon cacti, Prickly Pear cacti and Ocotillo bushes.

"Watch for snakes and scorpions," Snake warned.

The two men paralleled the driveway until they were adjacent to the mansion's guard shack and gated entrance. Snake pulled out some camouflage netting from his knapsack and handed some to Marty. They then laid prone on the desert ground and pulled the netting over themselves and began slowly crawling toward the gated entrance. They got to within thirty yards of the gate and lay prone on the ground under a large drooping Ocotillo bush, listening to the two guards chatting to each other. A light came on in the guard shack and occasionally Marty and Snake could hear traffic from the guard's portable radios. Suddenly a lot of talking back and forth began over the guards' portable radios, signaling something was happening. The sound of a helicopter was heard far off and getting closer. In a few minutes Snake and Marty heard a helicopter land inside the compound, but they were not able to see it. After things got quiet, Snake suggested they leave their position and climb a hill above the compound to see if they could achieve a better vantage point.

"Ouch!" Marty stated as they were crawling away under the camouflage netting.

"What happened?" Snake asked.

"I just got stung by a scorpion. Damn, it hurts."

Snake grabbed the scorpion and cut the stinger off its tail with his knife and put the scorpion in his mouth and began chewing and eating the arachnid.

"Oh my God. Are you eating that thing?" Marty asked.

"To let it go and not eat it would be unnatural. Marty,

I know you are a long way from New York City, but you have to understand something about your current environment," Snake remarked quietly looking into Marty's eyes. "You need to become part of this environment, not a visitor to it, or it will devour you in a million different ways. See that Prickly Pear cactus flower? Pick it gently and eat it," Snake instructed.

"I feel sick to my stomach, and I think that scorpion sting is affecting my vision," Marty stated as he picked the flower and began eating it.

"Let's just relax and lay here for a few minutes," Snake said while Marty ate the flower and picked another.

"It actually tastes kind of good," Marty mentioned as he lay chewing the flower.

"Let me see the sting."

Marty showed Snake his left forearm with a large red welt in the middle of his swollen arm.

"Hold it down and try not to elevate it and let me know if you start sweating," Snake stated as they packed up their camouflage netting and began hiking quietly in the dark up a hill to an area north of the compound.

"What does it mean if I start sweating?" Marty asked.

"It means you are a wimp-ass New Yorker and in need of pampering," Snake replied with a grin.

"Don't worry, scorpion bites are painful for up to 24 hours, but they are not deadly, unless of course you are allergic to them."

"I don't think I'm allergic to anything," Marty responded.

"Good, here's a claw. I saved it for you. Eat it. It's good," Snake said as Marty took the black scorpion claw and looked at it.

"When you eat it, as I explained before, you become more a part of the environment instead of a visitor to it," Snake pointed out.

"Can I wait until my stomach feels better?" Marty asked.

"Sure. It is up to you," Snake replied while they continued hiking up the hill.

"This is the twenty-two hundred hours check in," a voice crackled into the earphone of Marty's portable radio.

"Marty and Snake AOK. We had a helicopter land about an hour ago," Marty stated as he squeezed the transmit button on the portable radio.

"Lola and Annie AOK."

"Buck and Joe AOK. We have info that the target left the bar about 90 minutes ago for the airport."

Finally, "Hugo signing out and standing by for the ten hundred hours check-in tomorrow morning."

"Did you hear what Buck and Joe said?" Marty asked.

"Yes, it looks like Nicky may have left the bar, got a ride to the La Paz airport, and flew to the mansion via helicopter. It's the same helo we heard land here a while ago," Snake mentioned smiling as he looked over at Marty chewing on the scorpion claw.

After Marty finished eating the claw, Snake asked, "How are you feeling?"

"Better," Marty responded as he took a drink of water from the canteen.

"Can you help me understand something, Snake?" Marty asked.

"Anything, Marty. What is it?"

"Back at the Navy base, Captain Hugo contacted me and said several of his sailors saw you laying naked on the ground near the dormitory. They told him you were chanting something and chipping your teeth. They also said you had three rattlesnakes on you. One was wrapped around each of your arms and the third was coiled on your chest as you lay on your back on the ground, naked. Quite a story huh?" Marty asked.

"Yea, I didn't know anyone was watching. Sorry if it caused you some problems, sir," Snake responded.

"They went to get a camera and when they returned, they said you and the rattlers were gone. What were you doing?" Marty asked.

"It is difficult to explain to someone that doesn't understand, sir," Snake replied. "Laying naked on the ground allows my body to absorb some negative ions from the earth in this location. I am considered by the reptile world a brother to the snake and when I travel to a new area and have the time, I introduce myself to some of the local population. I also try to consume some of the local prey so that my body becomes part of the ecosystem instead of a stranger to it."

"I do not understand a word you just said, Snake, but you know what, it does not matter. If you believe something and need to act on your beliefs, however strange they might be to me, I have your back one hundred percent. You are a protector and caretaker Snake, and have given up much for your country to protect your people. I have the greatest respect for you," Marty responded. Snake smiled, while the tip of his tongue flicked in and out slightly between his teeth.

"This looks like a good spot to watch the compound. Let's gather some brush and pile it up and make ourselves a burrow so the morning sun will not expose us. Why don't you get comfortable, Marty, and try and get some rest until the morning check-in?" Snake suggested.

"OK, here is the radio and earpiece, Snake. Would you please wake me up before sunrise?"

"Sure, Marty, get some rest."

About two hours later Marty was awakened by a clicking sound.

"What's going on, what time is it?" Marty asked as he sat up.

"Sorry, Marty, I didn't mean to wake you. It is about 0430," Snake responded.

"What were you doing?" Marty asked.

"A Gila Monster came by and was curious what we were

up to, so I introduced myself. He wanted to hang around, but I explained we were hunting," Snake explained.

"A Gila Monster?"

"Yea, a chubby little guy, friendly though," Snake remarked.

As Snake was handing the portable radio and earpiece back to Marty a bright light appeared overhead causing the area to be as brightly lit as if it were daytime.

"What in the?" Marty mumbled.

Both men watched speechless as two glowing orbs danced in the dark sky overhead, hovering, then rotating over the compound without making a sound. The two glowing white orbs were about six feet in diameter, and they rotated opposite each other about fifty feet above the mansion in a clockwise, then counterclockwise manner. Marty took out the spotting scope, camera and tripod from his backpack, put it together, and began taking photos of the activity.

"Foo fighters. I wonder what they are doing here?" Snake asked just as someone from inside the mansion came out, pointed a rifle at the orbs and began firing.

The orbs immediately went straight up at tremendous speed and disappeared into the upper atmosphere.

"Keep down. I hope they didn't see us," Marty whispered quietly.

"I don't think so. The gunman was focused on the Foo Fighters."

"What was all that about?" Marty asked quietly after the gunman went back into the mansion.

"I think there is something bad about that compound. Something that has grabbed the attention of the Foo Fighters," Snake said as he prepared a place to curl up and sleep.

The sun came up in the east, bathing the peaks and canyons of the Sierra Giantas in a bright amber glow. Later, as the sun rose in the sky, warming the cool night air, the portable radio hissed.

"Ten hundred check-in," Captain Hugo's voice announced over the portable radio.

"AOK here in La Paz," responded Joe.

"AOK here in Agua Verde" responded Annie aboard SV Just Dandy with Lola.

"Some weird stuff here at the compound with Foo Fighters. They are gone now, all is AOK," Marty responded.

"Everyone has checked in AOK. Signing off and standing by until twenty-two hundred," Captain Hugo stated over the radio.

"What do you know about Foo Fighters?" Marty asked Snake.

"They were first reported by bomber pilots over Europe during WWII and also have been reported in India and in the Pacific, then later in Vietnam and many other places world-wide. My guess is they are interested in what we are doing with weapons of mass destruction. They seem to show up and check out anything or anybody that is in possession of WMD's or radioactive material," Snake said.

"We had a white cylindrical UFO follow us as we flew over Santa Rosalia on our way here. I wonder why they contacted the FBI aircraft. I don't think we have any WMD's in the plane's armory," Marty continued.

"No, but there are a several boxes of depleted uranium ammo aboard," Snake reported.

"Depleted uranium ammo?" Marty asked.

"Yes. It is called DU ammo. DU is much denser than lead and ignites upon impact so it has much better penetration for armor piercing and the combustible quality makes it a good weapon. DU is slightly radioactive and that could be the reason the Foo Fighters checked you out," Snake said.

"If that is the case, then I wonder what interest the Foo Fighters have in Pablo Escobar's mansion?" Marty asked.

"Good question," Snake responded as he got comfortable and prepared to get a little sleep.

Marty looked the mansion and grounds over carefully with the spotting scope while he listened to the others check in. Earlier that morning he saw the rising sun reflecting off the machine gun cartridges laying in the yard.

"Did you hear that?" Snake asked as he lifted his head from the ground. "It sounds like some trucks coming up the road."

A few minutes later a caravan of vehicles, led by an old school bus with faded yellow paint and the words "Santa Casa Iglesia" painted on the side, moved slowly up the driveway. The bus was filled with people of all ages and was driven by a priest wearing black clothing and a white priest's collar. Several pickup trucks and larger farm trucks followed the bus up the driveway to the guard shack and gate where they stopped and began honking their horns, yelling, whistling, and making noise.

The guards retreated to their shack and refused to open the gate. The priest drove ahead with the motor roaring, as if he was going to crash through the gate, at which time both guards left the guard shack and ran up the road toward the mansion. The helicopter started up and after a couple of minutes lifted off and flew toward the gate at a low altitude. It hovered just above the caravan causing dust and debris to be blown around in a big cloud. The caravan then began the difficult task of getting turned around on the narrow driveway so they could leave, while still honking their horns, yelling, and whistling. They slowly drove back down the driveway with the helicopter following.

"What was that all about?" Snake asked as Marty continued to watch the caravan through the spotting scope.

"My guess is the church people do not like Mr. Pablo Escobar very much," Marty stated.

"And it appears the feelings are mutual," Snake replied.

"I think it might be interesting speaking with that priest, Snake, what do you think?" Marty asked.

"The enemy of my enemy is my friend," Snake replied as they walked back toward the location where they had hidden their motorcycles.

"I want to talk to that priest and then I think we should report to the team at the next check in," Marty mentioned.

It was getting late as they rode back to Loreto and they both badly needed a shower, so Marty got them a room at the Hotel 1697 in the center of Loreto. Marty and Snake then went looking for the priest at the Santa Casa Church and found the faded yellow bus, with the words *Santa Casa Iglesia* written on its side, parked near the mission church near the center of Loreto. Marty found the priest in an office next to the mission church courtyard.

"*¿Hola, entiende Ingles Padre?*" Marty asked the priest.

"Yes, how can I help you?"

"Are you the priest that drives the yellow bus up to a ranch near San Javier?" Marty asked.

"Yes, why do you ask?"

"I can explain why I'm asking if I can get an assurance from you that you will keep our conversation to yourself."

"I will not keep important information unjustly hidden. Who are you?" the priest asked.

"I am Martin Goodson, a United States FBI Agent, and this is Snake, a retired soldier. We are interested in what is happening at the ranch you approached yesterday. But if word gets out about the FBI inquiring, we will have an even bigger problem than what is occurring now," Marty responded.

"You have my confidence Mr. Goodson. I am Miguel Papa, Jesuit, and pastor at the Santa Casa Church near here. Many of us in Loreto are concerned about the newly built rancho up near San Javier. Señor Pablo Escobar from Columbia brings his drug money and drug business here to this area so he can expand his business and corrupt our young people. We want him to leave, and we tell him so

in-person every time the Holy Spirt of Lights directs us,"
Father Papa stated.

"We gather at the church when we see the Holy Lights
and we make the trip to the ranch and demand he leave,"
Father Papa continued.

"We saw the lights. They appear to be UFOs. Where are
they from and what do they do?" Marty asked.

"We don't know for sure who or what they are, but many
believe they are the Holy Spirit of God sent here to help
us remove the evil that Pablo Escobar brings. They always
come from the north and return in the same direction."

"Father, I am not sure what is going to happen, but I am
helping the Mexican Navy with this problem. Please keep
this to yourself and please keep us in your prayers," Marty
asked.

"Peace be with you. I hope you are successful, and let
me know if I can help any further," Father Papa said as they
were about to part.

"May I have a moment alone with the priest, Marty?"

"Sure, Snake, I will meet you back at the room."

"Do you have a moment to hear my confession, Padre?"

"Sure, Señor Snake, have a seat in the confessional."

8.

SNAKE'S CONFESSION

"Please make yourself comfortable Señor Snake. May God bless you and give you the grace and humility to make a good confession and reconciliation with our Lord and Savior."

"Bless me Father, I confess that I have sinned. It has been over 35 years since my last confession, and these are my sins. The one's I can remember, at least."

"I killed 12 men during the Vietnam war, and probably more."

"I had relations with my Vietnamese girlfriend so many times, I cannot count."

"I skipped church on Sundays."

"This is going to take more than a few minutes, Father, I apologize," Snake muttered with a sheepish grin.

"Señor Snake, why don't we just say that for the past 35 years you have been living a life that was not congenial with God's love?"

"That sums it up Padre. But I'm not a bad person. I try but I don't always do the right thing."

"The lives you took during war were not sins as long as you believed it was a just war. The same would apply to a police officer who was trying to protect themselves or an innocent person from harm. Living as a married couple is another matter. Expressing your love physically is designed by God to be a very personal and loving act between two people who have made commitments and are responsible to each other in the sacrament of marriage. The estrangement from your Creator has caused your spirit to lack the grace of nourishment. The renewal with God will give you strength spiritually, physically, and emotionally. Your penance has already been mostly served in the scars I see on your face and arms Señor Snake, but I suggest you say a prayer before bed and as you awaken every day from now on, to remind you that God is with you always. Now pray the Act of Contrition."

"Oh my God, I am heartly sorry for having offended thee and I detest all my sins because I dread the loss of heaven and the pains of hell, but most of all because they offend thee my God who art all good and deserving of all my love. I firmly resolve, with the help of thy grace, to confess my sins, do penance, sin no more, and amend my life. Amen."

"The Almighty and merciful Lord God grants you indulgence, absolution and remission of your sins. Go in peace, Señor Snake, to love and serve the Lord."

Snake walked slowly to the tabernacle, knelt in prayer for a few minutes, and then returned to Padre Papa.

"Thank you, Father. Have you got a little more time to help me understand a promise I made to a priest a couple years ago?"

"Of course, Señor Snake. I will help you if I am able. What was the promise you made?"

"I promised a Catholic priest, like yourself, to keep something I saw and heard to myself. What I saw was very disturbing and it may have been a foresight into a horrible future. I want to warn the people I am working with about what the future may hold, but the promise I made will not allow it. The priest I made the promise to has since died. Does his death release me from my promise, Father?"

"Possibly. Why did the priest want the event kept secret?"

"He said he did not want panic to interfere with our work and said if we shared what we saw we would be ridiculed by some, but that many would fear the future."

"Tell me about what you saw and heard."

"I was detailed, with a partner named Sniffer, to assist and protect a Catholic priest in an exorcism of some old, secret, Chinese tunnels under a city up north. The circumstances that I experienced were not normal and as weird as anything I have seen in my entire life. During the exorcism the priest was saying prayers in Latin and using holy water and blessed oils. I didn't understand the ritual he was performing but I understood what happened in response. It was downright frightening, even for me after spending long periods of time in the Vietnamese tunnels. What happened was unbelievable."

"When we entered the tunnel, an eerie voice moaned and growled for a short period of time. We could not tell where the growl came from or what produced the putrid smells that were gagging us. Father Pat started praying loudly after we had walked about 50 yards into the main tunnel and at the same moment our flashlights failed. All three flashlights went dark on their own at the same time. We could not get them to work, and we were standing in the pitch-black tunnel unable to see our hands in front of our faces. Then a light came on. It was like a television screen about 20 feet in front of us. The screen had different colors dancing around until a small bright light flashed at the bottom of the screen and a blast of air hit us and almost knocked us off our feet. A mushroom cloud formed on the screen, and it was obvious we were watching a nuclear explosion. I then heard screaming and crying coming from off in the distance and we could smell burning flesh and saw people running with their clothes on fire, screaming. I passed out and everything went black. I woke up with Father Pat shaking me and we all had this fluffy ash-like substance covering us. We felt sick to our stomachs, and I had urinated on myself. We must have been out for some time since the team was worried about us and had been calling us on the radio. Father Pat said the demons were chased out of the tunnels, but we needed to clean the ash from ourselves with holy water. I took a shower when I got home but removing the black ash was impossible until I used holy water, the ash then washed away. Now, here on the Baja, we are trying to arrest a former drug detective and stop cartel activities and I think the apparition we saw in the tunnel a couple of years ago may contain a message that could help stop the attack, but I need to be released from my promise of secrecy, Father."

"I understand Señor Snake. I release you from your promise of secrecy to a brother priest and direct you to share the information with those who may benefit from it," Padre Papa stated.

"Thank you, Father."

"Go now, Señor Snake, with the Peace of Christ to do your duty, fortified with God's grace."

9.

SV Just Dandy

Annie and Lola's mission was to take Sailing Vessel Just Dandy south to the bay at Agua Verde and attempt to get word to Nicky and announce he is the father of Lola's unborn child with the hope of luring him into the open where he could be apprehended. Lola filled the boat's freshwater tanks and had the holding tank pumped out, the batteries checked and extra diesel fuel in jerry cans lashed to the foredeck. Provisions were also added to the sailboat's galley before they left. Annie walked barefoot to the foredeck and untied Just Dandy from the mooring ball in the harbor at Puerto Escondido while Lola checked the sailboat's small diesel motor to make sure sea water was circulating to cool the motor and was being expelled through the exhaust. After a couple of minutes, Lola slipped the boat's transmission into forward and motored the sailboat through the bay's entrance while watching the depth meter.

"When we get to Agua Verde, we will drop anchor and go ashore. I will contact Leona and see if she can get word to one of Pablo's men that I want to see Nicky, that I have some important news," Lola stated as she turned the bow of the sailboat north into the wind so the mainsail could be raised.

Lola held the boat's wheel, keeping it into the wind,

while Annie wrapped the halyard around a winch and began cranking the mainsail up the mast. Lola shut down the motor and Just Dandy fell off with the wind and began silently moving south toward Agua Verde. Annie then pulled the jib halyard to deploy the foresail, adding two knots to Just Dandy's smooth, quiet movement through the water.

"What a sweet boat," Annie remarked as Just Dandy continued moving quickly through the water making only the sound of the wake against her hull.

"She has been my home for three years and I love her," Lola said as she put the boat on autopilot and went down the companionway to the galley.

"Keep an eye on things would you Annie?" Lola yelled up from the galley. "She's on autopilot. I will make us something to eat and we can let Just Dandy sail herself while we enjoy lunch."

Annie sat back and relaxed, watching the scenery as Just Dandy sailed herself south toward Agua Verde. The Sea of Cortez was calm with a slowly, rolling swell out of the northeast and an 8-knot breeze out of the northwest, causing Just Dandy to sail lazily in a southerly direction.

It was late afternoon when they arrived just north of the entrance to Agua Verde. After starting the motor and checking again for sea water exiting the exhaust, Lola turned the sailboat around into the wind, facing north, and after rolling up the jib, released the stopper holding the mainsail's halyard. As the mainsail dropped between the lazy jacks, causing the sail to flake to the boom, Annie climbed up on deck and put ties around the sail, lashing it down to the boom. The two women then motored slowly into the bay as Lola scanned the area with her binoculars. They were alone, with no other boats anchored in the bay, so Lola motored over to the northeast corner of the bay, just off a sandy beach that had a small vacant cottage up above the waterline. Just to the north, at the shore, were the sea caves where

Nicky killed two Mexican sailors. Lola dropped anchor by engaging the electric windlass at a depth of twenty feet. She let out a hundred feet of chain and slowly backed Just Dandy up until the anchor dug deep into the sandy bottom. She shut down the diesel motor and took a deep breath, watching the boat for a while to make sure the anchor was holding firm.

"Let's make a nice supper, have a glass of wine and relax this evening. We can wait to go ashore tomorrow morning," Annie suggested.

"That sounds fine with me. Maybe Leona will be at her beach restaurant, and we can have breakfast there," Lola responded.

Lola put a couple of potatoes in the microwave and cut up some lettuce, avocado, onion, and opened a can of black olives for a salad. Annie got the barbecue started to grill two steaks. The table was set in the cockpit with a bottle of a Mexican Gato Negro Reserve cabernet wine with two glasses, napkins, silverware, and salad dressing. Lola opened the bottle and poured wine into the glasses, handing a glass to Annie.

"Thank you. It will be a few minutes before the steaks are ready," Annie said.

"That gives us a little time to work on the bottle of cabernet," Lola responded with a smile.

"My, what a lifestyle. I love it. How did you get mixed up with a guy like Nicky?" Annie asked as she took a drink of wine.

"I grew up in the village of Agua Verde. We were very poor, but we got a good basic education, and we were happy. I wanted more. I wanted to be rich like the movie stars and when Nicky arrived with a pocket full of money, I thought he was sent from heaven. I learned, too late, that he was sent from the depths of *el infierno*."

After supper, as the sun was setting behind the tall

Sierra's, painting some light, leafy clouds a soft pink color, Annie mentioned, "It is difficult to imagine anyone wanting to be violent in such a beautiful environment."

A school of baitfish swam toward the anchored sailboat while a pod of dolphins chased the school and pelicans dove on the baitfish from the air. After watching the activity for a few minutes as darkness approached, the two women retired to the salon to watch a recorded movie on the TV, taking the unfinished bottle of wine with them. Before retiring, Lola went to the sailboat's instrument panel above the chart table and turned on the anchor light, which was at the top of Just Dandy's mast.

The next morning Annie, asleep in the V-berth, woke to the sound of the electric freshwater pump as Lola filled the coffee pot. Peeking out from the V-berth in the bow, Annie was greeted by Lola smiling at her from the galley.

"How'd you sleep?" Lola asked.

"Like a log. I hope that wine didn't make me snore."

"No, I didn't hear you snoring, but I did hear some whales calling out at about three AM. The berth in the aft stateroom is below the waterline and I occasionally hear the whales talking to each other. It's pretty cool to get up on a night with a full moon and see them feeding on krill in the bay," Lola remarked.

"The stars last night were the brightest I've ever seen them." Annie said.

"The coffee will be ready in a few minutes, Annie. Then we can take the dinghy ashore and see if we can find Leona at the beach restaurant."

While sitting in the cockpit finishing their coffee Annie told Lola, "I have a pistol in my backpack, and I carry a large folding knife in my pocket for protection. Are you carrying any weapons?"

"No, I have nothing," Lola lied. "But I do know how to shoot if it is necessary. Let me put a few pumps of air in the inflatable dinghy since it looks like it deflated a little during the cool night, then we can go ashore."

It was about a mile dinghy ride to Leona's beach restaurant. There were two four-wheel drive pickups with campers parked on the beach that had made the forty-kilometer trek on a dirt trail through the mountains. There were also three tents on the beach with two motorcycles parked nearby. Next to the restaurant were two smaller temporary plywood structures. One had a hand-written sign on it stating, *"Baño 1 Peso"* The other structure also had a handwritten sign stating, *"Shower 2 Peso"*.

Leona, the proprietor, was in a rear sectioned off area of the restaurant cooking breakfast for a young couple seated at one of the tables. Annie and Lola took a seat at the second table and greeted the young couple. Leona's husband, Enrique, approached the table and greeted Lola and Annie with a smile and some welcoming words in Spanish. Lola asked Enrique for breakfast for two with coffee in Spanish, and Leona came out from the kitchen when she heard Lola's voice and gave her a hug. Lola whispered to Leona she needed to talk privately with her when she had a chance and Leona nodded before she returned to the kitchen. After breakfast, and when the young couple had left, Lola privately explained to Leona she wanted to get word to Nicky that she was pregnant with his child and wanted to speak with him. Lola told her it was urgent that she speak with Nicky as soon as possible. Leona agreed to pass the word but made no promises.

Lola started the dinghy motor to return to Just Dandy after they walked the shoreline for a while. Annie swam while Lola slowly motored the dinghy, following Annie back to Just Dandy. They spent the rest of the day and the next day swimming, snorkeling, and fishing while waiting for word from Nicky.

Annie was prepared to take Nicky into custody if she

could get the drop on him. She kept her backpack with the pistol, knife, and handcuffs always close by. On the second day in the late afternoon a helicopter came in from the north and circled the bay at a low altitude. It then hovered over Just Dandy causing sea spray to fly around from the wash from the rotor. It then moved several hundred yards away and hovered, facing Just Dandy.

"Just Dandy, Just Dandy, Nicolas calling," came the call over the sailboat's VHF radio on channel sixteen.

"Just Dandy, Just Dandy, Nicolas calling," again crackled the VHF radio.

"Just Dandy, go ahead Nicky," Lola responded.

"Go to channel 68," came the response.

Lola turned the radio to channel 68 and called, "Nicky, Nicky, Just Dandy, go ahead."

"I got your message. You need to take care of business and I will provide the doctor. Meet me at Ensenada de los Muertos in three days and I will have everything ready for you," Nicky demanded.

"I can make Los Muertos in three days only if I have good winds. How about five days?" Lola asked over the radio while the helicopter hovered, still facing the sailboat at about two hundred yards distance.

"OK, five days. This better happen Lola. I don't want any loose ends out there to cause me problems, understand?" Nicky warned over the radio as the helicopter rose in the air and flew south.

"Leave your swim ladder down for me," Nicky stated as the helicopter disappeared on the horizon.

Lola sat at the chart table with the radio's microphone still in her hand, weeping quietly.

He is going to kill me, she whispered to herself.

10.

La Paz, Baja México

Joe and Buck caught a ride from the Navy base at Puerto Escondido to the Loreto Airport where they rented a car for a drive to La Paz México. They checked on FBI Agents Jack Rosen and Hank Carter guarding the jet aircraft before driving to La Paz. Two Mexican Navy sailors stopped Joe and Buck as they approached the cordoned off aircraft. Jack and Hank looked out and greeted them from the doorway of the aircraft.

"*¡Gracias, amigos!*" Hank yelled to the sailors as Joe and Buck climbed the stairs to the aircraft.

"Are you guys going a little stir crazy?" Joe asked the two men.

"I have run out of crossword puzzles to do and all he talks about is drinking a cold beer when he knows we can't drink on the job," Jack replied.

"How would you guys like to have a good steak dinner and maybe a beer, on me?" Joe asked.

"Are you kidding? We were just discussing where we would go if we went AWOL," Hank responded, smiling.

"I know a great steak house in Loreto, and I think we can take a break for a couple hours if we can get Buck to stand in for you here," Joe suggested.

"I would be happy to do that. It will give me a chance to

check the aircraft systems and make sure everything is ready to go, if necessary," Buck responded.

"I heard about this steak house in Loreto called Domingo's and I have an idea where it's at. When you're ready we can drive into Loreto and see if we can find it," Joe said.

"There's plenty of food in the galley Buck, if you get hungry," Jack said.

"Thanks, Jack. Have a good time you guys," Buck responded as Jack, Hank and Joe left the aircraft.

"*¿Me voy a Loreto, Puedo traerte algo?*" Joe asked a Mexican sailor if there was anything he needed.

"*Nada, gracias amigo.*" The sailor responded with a smile.

"Hey where did you learn the Spanish?" Hank asked.

"On the street. I was a foot patrolman for 8 years, but don't count on me speaking perfect Spanish," Joe replied.

The three-mile drive to Loreto crossed two dry washes. The summer rains fill the washes with water rushing down from the mountains to the Sea of Cortez, but they usually dry up during the winter. Joe found Domingo's Restaurant just after turning off Mexican Highway 1 into Loreto Village.

"The waiter is asking how you want your steak cooked," Joe mentioned to Hank and Jack after being seated in an outdoor courtyard next to a small waterfall.

"Gee, what a nice place, Joe, thanks for thinking of us. I would like my steak medium rare," Jack announced.

"Same with me," Hank replied.

"*Dos cuatros para nosotros,*" Joe told the waiter as bottles of Pacifico beer were placed in front of them.

"*Mil Islas y Queso azul,*" Joe responded when the waiter asked what kind of salad dressings they wanted.

"You didn't learn that walking the beat," Hank remarked about Joe speaking Spanish.

"No, I learned that when I got hungry," Joe responded as they all laughed.

The two-inch thick rib eye steaks were seared and sizzling

on the outside and pink in the middle.

"Just perfect, my steak could not be better. I do need another beer to help wash it down.

"*Otra cerveza, por favor,*" Jack asked the waiter. "I am learning some important Spanish words myself," Jack said as they all laughed again.

The meal was pleasant and the drive back to the airport was quiet as the men adjusted their attitudes back to completing their missions.

"Thanks, Joe. We sure appreciate the break in the routine," Jack said as they walked toward the jet aircraft.

"It was my pleasure, gentlemen, I appreciate the boring work you are doing, keeping the aircraft safe," Joe replied. "By the way, if you are looking for something else to do that might break the boredom, there is one thing."

"Anything you need Joe, you got it," Jack responded with Hank nodding.

"You see Mexican highway 1 over there?"

"Yes, we can easily see the highway from here," Hank said.

"The intersection where the road to the airport meets Mexican highway 1 is something that could use keeping an eye on. That is the road up to San Javier and Pablo Escobar's mansion. From what Marty and Snake tell us, Pablo and Nicky either come and go to the compound via helicopter or by two black four-wheel drive Chevy Suburbans, driving in tandem. It would be helpful if we knew when Pablo and Nicky were on the move by watching for the helicopter or the Suburbans."

"No problem. We can place one of our wireless alerts just west of the intersection and it can notify us whenever a vehicle breaks the beam," Hank said.

"So, you want to know if we see the helicopter or the black Chevy Suburbans on the move, right?" Jack asked.

"Yes, that would be really helpful," Joe responded.

"We have seen that helicopter getting fuel here at the

airport, so we are familiar with it. Only the pilot is aboard when he gets fuel," Jack mentioned.

"OK, well Joe and I are headed for La Paz so we can hang out at a bar and watch TV," Buck said with a grin.

"Some guys have all the luck," Hank responded as the men parted.

Their mission was to attempt to locate Nicky possibly at the Tailhunter Restaurant and Bar where he is reported to watch Seattle Seahawk games. La Paz is the capital city of the State of Baja Sur, México. Baja Sur takes in the southern half of the Baja Peninsula including the popular resort city of Cabo San Lucas.

It is close to an eight-hour drive by car from Loreto to La Paz, passing through a score of dusty Mexican fishing and farming villages. The two-lane gravel road was used extensively by large semi-trucks, farm trucks, pickups, cars, horses, motorcycles, bicycles, mule drawn carts, and pedestrians. It was not uncommon to see horses and cows standing or laying in the roadway during their trip. It was dark by the time they reached the farm town of Ciudad Constitution about a hundred miles South of Loreto.

"Hotel Conquistador looks inviting Buck, what do you think?" Joe asked.

"I could use a good night's sleep," Buck responded as Joe pulled to a stop in front of the hotel.

The next morning, after fresh showers, Joe and Buck found breakfast at a nearby restaurant that opened at 6 AM.

"This is definitely a farm town," Buck stated while waiting at 7 AM to get a table.

They were on their way to La Paz by 8 AM, traveling south on Mexican highway 1 for another six hours before they passed the large propane facility on the outskirts of La Paz. La Paz was active and busy, the streets were clean, and people were going about their business just the same as any other medium sized city in the world. La Paz was not a rich city, but it was orderly and peaceful, and the people seemed friendly. Joe drove the rented car down to the bay and followed the bayside drive to La Perla Hotel on the waterfront.

"Hotel La Perla opened in 1940 and has been in operation since, according to this brochure," Joe mentioned while checking in at the front desk.

"¿Donde esta La Tailhunter Cantina?" Joe asked the clerk.

"Let's take a walk to the Tailhunter Bar after we check out our room. We can then find out when the Seahawks play next and look the place over," Buck suggested after they got directions.

"Sounds good," Joe replied.

The bayside promenade, or malecón as it is called in Spanish, was several miles long and wide enough for several people to walk side by side along the large bay. A two-lane paved street paralleled the malecón where numerous restaurants, bars, ice cream shops, bicycle, motorcycle, and car rental agencies faced the beach. Palm trees, palapas or palm thatched shade structures and benches lined the beach along with playground equipment for children. Several large open skiffs, called *pangas* in Spanish, with outboard motors lined the beach accompanied by the skippers, or *pangueros*, waiting to take tourists out to the islands or to swim with the whale sharks in La Paz Bay.

"Whale sharks are the largest fish in the world. They are not dangerous as they are filter feeders and are very placid. People enjoy swimming with the whale sharks which can reach forty feet in length," the hotel clerk explained.

The three story Tailhunter Restaurant and Bar faces the malecón and La Paz Bay about four blocks North of La Perla Hotel. The top floor, with its open-air windows facing west, provides the best view of activity on the bay and the malecón and faces the beautiful sunsets for which La Paz is known. Each floor of the restaurant and bar has several television sets tuned to different sporting events.

Many people from Washington, Oregon, California and British Columbia, Canada have traditionally spent time on the Baja during the winter, some bringing with themselves a passion for the newly formed Seattle Seahawks professional football team. The feelings of support many fans had for the Seahawks football team overrode their good sense, causing them to paint their faces with the team colors, wear outlandish clothing, and act in a bizarre manner, showing support for their team. Many locals from La Paz and the resort city of Cabo San Lucas also began following the football team prompting a local television station to broadcast the games, narrated in Spanish.

"Is Pacifico beer OK, Buck?" Joe asked.

"Pacifico beer is fine," Buck replied.

"*Dos Pacificos y un menú, por favor,*" Joe stated to the waiter.

"There's a Seahawks game scheduled for the day after tomorrow at 6 PM," Joe reported after looking at the schedule posted on the wall under the television set.

"*¿Estara el juego de football de los Seahawks en television, en dos días, no?*" Joe asked the waiter.

"*Si, Seahawks aqui,*" the waiter responded verifying the posted schedule.

"We should get here early so we can pick a good seat to observe the crowd. I don't think we want to make the arrest unless there is an easy opportunity. If Nicky shows up, we can see where he sits, how many are with him, and determine if we can plan an assault for the next Seahawks game. Nicky is acquainted with me so I will try to stay away from him, and I'll change my appearance," Joe said.

The two men finished their meals of freshly caught shrimp and fish, then walked back toward their hotel.

"That ice cream looks good," Joe remarked as they approached an ice cream shop on the *malecón*. They sat on a bench overlooking the bay watching the changing colors of the sunset while finishing their ice cream cones.

"What do you think about renting a *panga* for the day tomorrow and doing some exploring of the local waters?" Joe asked.

"I think it is a good idea, Joe. We need to know the lay of the land if we are going to be making an arrest here," Buck agreed.

The next morning, after breakfast at La Perla Restaurant, Joe and Buck took a walk along the *malecón* to look over the *pangas* and the *pangueros*.

"Look at that *panga*. It has two seventy-five horsepower outboard motors, and the skipper is an older fellow who looks like he knows these waters well. Let's check him out," Buck suggested.

Joe spoke with the *panguero* in broken Spanish and the gentleman responded in fairly good English.

"He says he will take us wherever we want to go, and it will cost us fifty dollars US for eight hours."

"Sounds good," Buck replied.

"The skipper's name is Ramon Rodriguez. He says he is retired from fishing," Joe said with a smile.

"I take care of my family by fishing for thirty years. I sleep in fish camps many nights and I go through many storms and nearly drown," Ramon explained. "But I feed my family because God blesses me with many fish. I think about running *mota* North because they pay many dollars. But that bad business. Bad business cause too many problem. Now, my kids raised, and they move out. So, I retire, make little money from tourist."

"What's *mota*?" Buck asked.

"That is one of their words for marijuana," Joe stated.

"Si, *mota* not so bad, but cartel very bad. Where we go today?" Ramon asked as they waded to the *panga* and climbed aboard.

Another *panguero* pushed the boat off the beach and Ramon started the outboard motors and slowly backed away, then turned and headed slowly north.

"Take us where you take the tourists," Joe asked.

At a point opposite the city pier Ramon turned the *panga* east and crossed the large sand bar headed for the bay near the sandy peninsula called the *Magote*.

Ramon slowed the *panga* down and said, "Look into the water to see whale sharks."

Two whale sharks were swimming just below the surface side by side. Both had large, open mouths as they swam slowly through the water. They were dark colored with light colored spots and the larger fish was longer than the thirty-foot *panga*.

"Amazing!" Buck exclaimed as they continued to watch the fish.

After a while Ramon turned northwest and headed for *Isla Espiritu Santo* (Holy Spirit Island). Ramon got Buck and Joe's attention by pointing out a pod of whales.

They got a little closer and Ramon exclaimed, "Fin whale, big!"

One whale swam next to the *panga* and was about twice the length of the thirty-foot boat. The whale then went under the *panga* and began swimming on the other side, rising up to take a look at the men in the boat, before it swam away.

Ramon took his tourists into *Bahia San Gabriel* and several of the other bays as they explored the west side of *Isla Espiritu Santo*. They went into *Caleta Partida*, a bay that offered protection from winds out of almost every direction. The clear water allowed them to see the bottom at thirty feet and the remote, white sandy beaches beckoned them to explore. At the north end of the island, they came upon a rocky outcrop with a sea lion rookery. The grunts and barks of the sea lions welcomed the *panga* as it drew near. One large bull sea lion made a unique sound that was nothing like a bark but more of a long, loud growl or grunt.

"He the big bull," Ramon stated as he turned the *panga* east.

Ramon took the *panga* down the east side of *Isla Espiritu*

Santo past Bonanza Beach and across the strait to *La Ventana* (the window) and *Ensenada de Los Muertos* (bay of the dead) and back toward La Paz and Balandra Beach and the locally famous Mushroom Rock. Ramon motored down the long channel to the center of the *malecón* where he beached the *panga* and shut down the motors.

"Thank you, Ramon, that was a nice day," Joe said as he handed Ramon a ten-dollar tip.

"Thank you, gentlemen. Here is me *tarjeta*, call me if you need anything," Ramon stated handing a business card to Joe as he tied his *panga* to a block of cement on the beach.

On their walk back to the room at La Perla Hotel Joe said, "I think we should take a trip out to the La Paz airport and take a look around before Nicky arrives tomorrow."

"We can do that after supper tonight if you like, Joe," Buck responded.

"OK, let's take a cab to the Mesquite Grill for supper and then out to the airport to have a look after we change clothes back at our room," Joe suggested.

"I've heard about this place," Buck mentioned.

"I have too, and I can't wait to try one of their steaks," Joe responded.

After cleaning up and changing clothes, Joe approached a taxi driver parked in front of the hotel. "*¿Cuanto a la Mesquite Grill?*" Joe asked the driver.

"Four pesos for a ride to the Mesquite Grill," the driver responded in English as they got in the cab.

The Mesquite grill was a small, partially open-air restaurant with the kitchen and grill in the front next to the entrance. Joe ordered a rib eye steak, medium rare, and a hamburger for Buck in Spanish. The two men chatted about their expected encounter with Nicky tomorrow.

"I don't think we should try to take him tomorrow even if it looks inviting to do so. We should have the whole team present when we make our move, and we should have plans

B and C ready to go if plan A fails," Joe declared.

"I agree," Buck responded.

Arriving by taxi at the La Paz airport they learned private aircraft parking was located at the north end of the field and no helicopter was observed, so they headed back to their room for the evening.

The next morning, they took turns keeping an eye on the sky to the north hoping to see Nicky and Pablo arriving by helicopter from the mansion near Loreto. Joe had let his hair grow longer after leaving the Yakima Police Department and he also grew a short beard so disguising himself from Nicky was not that difficult. Joe also wore a baseball cap which he pulled down over his sunglasses.

"You look like a beach bum," Buck said.

"I guess that was a compliment," Joe responded as they both laughed. "Let's get there about four thirty so we can get a seat that lets us see the crowd as much as possible."

Just after arriving at the Tailhunter, Joe and Buck spotted a helicopter flying toward La Paz from the north.

"That is a Messerschmitt 105 helicopter. That must be Pablo and Nicky," Buck said as they watched the helicopter turn towards the La Paz airport.

"We should see Nicky in the next thirty minutes," Joe said as he looked north at traffic on the *malecón*, towards the airport.

"We should easily see them when they show up at the entrance downstairs from here," Joe said as they sat at the table in the open veranda facing the bay.

"Why don't we separate before Nicky gets here so they don't think we are together," Joe suggested.

Buck moved to a table across the room which was beginning to fill up with Seahawk fans. Joe watched a taxi van pull up in front at the entrance and saw five men get out.

There is Nicky, Joe thought to himself as Nicolas James Cabot got out from the right front seat of the taxi van.

Four young Hispanic men got out from the rear of the van and Joe watched as they readjusted their firearms under their shirts.

Those young men can't be over eighteen, Joe thought to himself as he looked at Buck across the room.

When he saw Buck looking at him, Joe gave a nod indicating Nicky's arrival. Two of Nicky's bodyguards climbed the circular iron staircase to the second floor of the Tailhunter ahead of Nicky and two followed. Nicky took a seat immediately with his back to the wall at a table that had a reserved sign on it. With four bodyguards surrounding him, Nicky leaned back in his chair, stretched, and then ordered a pitcher of Tecate beer for everyone at the table. Joe and Buck watched the table while attempting not to appear interested. Nicky drank one beer after another while the young bodyguards drank very little. Joe noticed that each bodyguard watched people closely while watching the television and keeping an eye out for any possible threats against Nicky. Nicky looked pretty much the same, a little older maybe. He was dressed in jeans, a colorful Hawaiian shirt, and loafers and appeared slightly tipsy. After the game finished, with the Seahawks beating the Denver Broncos, Nicky paid the bill to the waiter at the table in pesos, and he was then escorted down the stairs to the sidewalk in the front of the bar where a bodyguard flagged down a taxi.

"That was interesting," Buck mentioned to Joe as people were leaving.

"There would have been a lot of collateral damage if we had tried to take him today," Joe responded.

"I agree. I think each one of those bodyguards was packing a gun. It would have been a big shootout for sure."

Thirty minutes later a helicopter was seen flying north from the La Paz airport towards Loreto and San Javier.

"When is the next game?" Joe asked as he looked at the schedule posted on the wall. "One week from today, same place, same time," remarked Joe answering his own question. "I will share what we saw tonight during the 10 PM check in."

11.

THE ARREST PLAN

"Hello, *Hola*, my name is Madison Gardner, *mi nom-bre…*" FBI Special Projects Agent Madison Gardner said over the telephone to the Mexican Naval Facility at Puerto Escondido from her headquarters office in Washington, DC.

"Yes, this is Captain Hugo Chávez of the Mexican Navy, how can I help you?"

"I am trying to contact FBI Agent Martin Goodson."

"He is in the field now. May I ask him to return your call?"

"Yes, please ask him to call me on the STU phone."

"Does he have that phone number?" Hugo asked.

"Yes, please ask him to contact me as soon as possible. Thank you, sir," Madison replied before the call ended.

About an hour later Marty and Snake arrived, riding their motorcycles.

"Welcome back Marty. How did it go? You missed a phone call from Agent Madison Gardner at FBI Headquarters. She said it was important," Hugo stated.

"We learned a lot, Hugo. Let me call Madison back and I will fill you in on what we found."

"Madison asked you to use the STU phone," Hugo added.

"Oh, OK. I will need to get it hooked up. It should only

take a few minutes. Let me explain what Snake and I found during our reconnoiter of Pablo Escobar's compound while I get this STU phone connected."

"The compound is very secure with a nine-foot-tall fence and concertina wire surrounding the compound's several acres. There is a guard shack and a gate at the entrance with armed security and at least two other armed guards inside the compound at all times. The helicopter comes and goes, and we observed two black Chevrolet four-wheel drive Suburbans parked next to the main house. Two things happened while we watched the compound," Marty explained. "First, after dark some Foo Fighters came by and circled the compound, then hovered over the compound until the guards began shooting at them. They were about six feet in diameter and glowed a bright white. They rotated in a circle opposite each other and went over the entire compound without making a sound until the guards started shooting, then they disappeared straight up into the sky. Snake calls them Foo Fighters," Marty continued.

"The next morning a church bus, filled with about fifty people, came up the driveway, with Father Papa driving. There were cars and trucks following the bus honking their horns, yelling, chanting, and making a lot of noise. They stopped at the gate to the compound where they were refused entrance. As they were turning around to leave, a helicopter took off from inside the compound and hovered over the caravan, causing dust to swirl around them. The caravan turned around and left, and the helicopter flew off to the south," Marty explained.

"Snake and I stopped at the mission church in Loreto where we found the priest that drove the bus. I talked to him about what he was doing at the compound. He said Pablo Escobar is engaged in the illegal drug trade and he is bringing big problems to the Baja and the priest wants him to leave," Marty said.

Marty then called Madison on the STU phone.

"Hello, Madison is that you?" Marty asked.

"Yes, this is Madison. Who is calling please?" Madison asked.

"Hi Madison, it's Marty Goodson."

"Oh, hi, Marty. Thanks for calling. Your voice sounds like it has an echo," Madison said.

"Yes, it is probably because our voices are being encrypted," Marty explained.

"Marty, I have some information which I think is important to your mission."

"What is it, Madison, go ahead please."

"I am not sure if I should be sharing this information since I discovered it in areas I am not normally authorized to be inspecting."

"Let's just keep this between you and me for the time being. It may not affect our mission here in which case we don't need to say anything."

"OK Marty, I trust you and I just want to warn you about some other government operations being conducted which may affect your mission. The CIA has something going on in México that has their attention, and the DEA has agents in the field conducting an operation near you. Please don't ask me how I know this."

"Don't worry, Madison. I will check it out by having my supervisor see what is happening and I promise to keep your name out of it. I owe you, Maddy – Thank you," Marty said before the call ended.

"Boy, this is getting complicated," Marty mentioned to Hugo.

"I will call my supervisor and try to find out what else is going down on the Baja that we don't know about," Marty said as he started dialing the STU phone.

"Meanwhile, let's get everybody together, Hugo. We need to have a team meeting so we can determine a course of action and get Nicky in custody to complete our mission."

"I can ask them to report to a central location like San Evaristo where SV Hannah is anchored with Captain Kirk."

"That sounds good."

At the 10 PM check-in Annie reported the contact with Nicky and the agreement to meet him at Muertos Bay in 5 days. Hugo asked Annie and Lola to sail south the next morning for a team meeting and meet up with SV Hannah and Captain Kirk Christian, who was at anchor in the bay at San Evaristo.

"Agua Verde is 44 nautical miles north of San Evaristo and, with a breeze from the north, SV Just Dandy should make the trip in about 8 hours averaging five knots per hour," Hugo explained to Annie.

Joe and Buck were asked to find a *panga* to take them north 51 nautical miles to San Evaristo for the team meeting aboard SV Hannah.

"A *panga* should take less than three hours to get to San Evaristo from La Paz. See you tomorrow. I've contacted everybody except Snake. You and I will head for San Evaristo tomorrow for the team meeting. I will have our *panga* readied for us to take to San Evaristo tomorrow morning. It is unmarked and looks like a working fishing *panga*, so we won't attract attention. It is about seventy nautical miles to San Evaristo from Puerto Escondido so it will take us about four hours," Hugo reported.

"OK then, all I need now is a return call from my supervisor to see if there is something going on that we need to know about. Let's grab some supper, Hugo, and wait for a call back on the STU phone. Where is Snake?" Marty asked.

"I saw him with Lieutenant Veronica earlier," Hugo responded.

"I guess if Snake gets hungry, he will be able to help himself," Marty quipped.

"I have no doubt Mr. Snake knows how to take care of himself," Hugo replied with a slight grin.

"If you see him, would you let him know we are going to San Evaristo tomorrow morning?" Marty asked.

"Sure, Marty, but my guess is he is spending some time with Lieutenant Veronica at her apartment. It is on the second floor at the end, number 207."

"OK, I will stop by there after supper if I don't see him sooner."

While taking supper in the mess hall a sailor came running into the room and up to Captain Hugo. Captain Hugo returned the salute and asked what he needed.

"*Suena el teléfono especial.*"

"Your STU phone is calling," Hugo translated as Marty got up and quickly left the table.

"*Gracias,*" Marty responded as he walked out the door to answer the STU phone.

After speaking with his supervisor on the encrypted telephone, Marty went looking for Snake to let him know they would be traveling to San Evaristo Bay early the next morning. As he approached apartment 207, he noticed the shade was partially open on the window and he could see Snake without a shirt and a woman with long dark hair in front of Snake bending over.

"Show it to me please, let me see all of it. Oh, my God, I can't believe it," the woman was yelling at Snake.

Maybe I should come back later, Marty thought to himself.

"You have the longest one, *mi serpiente,* "the woman said.

"Who's there?" Snake asked loudly.

"It's me, Marty, sorry to disturb you."

"It's OK, Marty. Come in please," Snake responded as he put on a shirt.

"You know Lieutenant Veronica Sabroso already don't you, sir?"

"Yes, of course. Nice to see you, Lieutenant," Marty stated.

"Welcome, Señor Marty. We were just looking at Señor Snake's scars from the Vietnam War. He is the most amazing man.

The scar on his stomach must be ten inches long!" she exclaimed.

"I just wanted to let you know we will be leaving after breakfast tomorrow morning, Snake," Marty explained, looking a little embarrassed.

"OK, sir, I will see you at breakfast. Good night, sir."

"I want to see you back," Lieutenant Veronica said to Snake as she pulled on his shirt.

Marty left the two to themselves. The next morning after breakfast Captain Hugo had a 30-foot *panga* with two one hundred horsepower Mercury outboard motors on the stern ready to make a fast trip to San Evaristo Bay. It was another sunny winter day with temperatures reaching eighty degrees during the day and dropping to the high fifty degrees Fahrenheit at night. The *panga* had a Bimini top to protect the occupants from the bright sun. Hugo motored slowly through the narrow passage leading to the open Sea of Cortez and turned the boat south and slowly increased speed.

The water was flat, due to calm conditions during the night, but there was a three-foot swell coming from the north and moving peacefully in a southerly direction, the result of a windstorm two days prior. After the *panga* got up to speed, it would climb a swell and then surf down the far side of the swell, which was moving in the same direction, as they made their way to San Evaristo.

"We should see Just Dandy with Annie and Lola sailing south from Agua Verde as we head for San Evaristo. How will Joe and Buck get to San Evaristo?" Hugo asked.

"They will hire a *panga* from La Paz this morning," Marty responded.

"So, Annie, Lola, Joe, Buck, Snake, you and I will be meeting aboard SV Hannah with Captain Kirk?" Hugo asked.

"Yes, plus two other people," Marty answered.

"Two other people?" Hugo and Snake asked in unison.

"Yes, I will explain in detail when we get together aboard SV Hannah later, but we will also be meeting with a Drug

Enforcement Administration (DEA) agent and a Central Intelligence Agency (CIA) agent," Marty advised.

DEA and CIA agents. I wonder what is up? Snake thought to himself.

There was a pause with little conversation as the serious turn of the mission began to weigh on them.

Later, Marty said to Snake, "I apologize for intruding on you and Lieutenant Veronica last night."

"You weren't intruding, Marty. She just wanted to see my scars. I know that sounds a little crazy, sir, but she is an amazing person. She believes the greatest thing a person can do in life is to protect their loved ones, and she has great respect for people that risk their lives and suffer for the sake of others. She considers a scar received in battle for the protection of others a badge of honor. She wanted to know about my service to the United States, so I told her, and she said she has hopes that she will be able to show her love for her country and her people someday in a similar manner. She is also a courageous and incredible woman," Snake stated.

"She is one of the Mexican Navy's most important assets, besides being an astounding person," Hugo responded. "I couldn't help but overhear you, Snake. You are exactly right, she is a unique person, I'm sure she would not mind if I shared some of her history."

"Yes, please," Snake responded.

"She was raised near here at a small fishing village called Juncalito. Her father was a fisherman, a very dangerous occupation, and she has six older brothers. She is an only daughter because her two older sisters took sick and died when they were young. Growing up, she worked with her father and brothers fishing the Sea of Cortez for several years. She attended the Catholic school in Loreto and graduated with honors. Later, two of her brothers were lost at sea during a fishing trip, and because of that, she decided to become a sailor to help protect Mexican fishermen. She later graduated with honors from the Mexican Naval Academy and attained rank quickly, working at the naval base in Manzanillo. Lieutenant Veronica was transferred here a year ago and has fit in very nicely," Hugo continued.

"A few months ago, she welcomed three new recruits who had just graduated from the Mexican Naval Academy and were assigned to her squad here at the Puerto Escondido Naval Base. The next weekend she invited the three to celebrate their graduation and new assignments. They went to El Condor Cantina in Loreto and engaged in a night of drinking the nectar of the Blue Agave. Later that night one of the recruits made a feminist joke and she responded with an insulting joke of her own, and things went downhill from there. It turned physical and Lieutenant Veronica proceeded to beat the *caca* out of all three recruits. Growing up with six brothers may have given her an advantage. She then had the local police transport them to the naval base here and placed all three in the brig. The next morning, she went to the brig and released them after apologies were exchanged. She agreed not to press formal charges against the three and instead sent them out with shovels to dig a ditch. They not only dug the ditch, while trying to recover from the previous evening, but they also made the ditch twice as long and twice as deep as she requested. Lieutenant Veronica is greatly respected and loved by everyone at this base and her squad would follow her through the gates of hell if asked," Hugo remarked.

"What a superb asset for the Mexican people," Marty said.

"What an exceptional person," Joe responded.

The *panga* developed a rhythm, slowing as it climbed a southbound swell, then increasing in speed as the *panga* reached the top of the swell and began running down the backside. One swell after another put the *panga* into a repeating process of climbing the next swell and surfing down the far side as the trip wore on past Honeymoon Cove, Isla

Dazante, Isla Monserrat and then finally, Agua Verde Bay.

"Do you see SV Just Dandy in the bay at Agua Verde?" Marty asked Hugo.

"No, there are no boats at anchor in Agua Verde. Annie and Lola are probably an hour ahead of us on their way to Bahia San Evaristo and we may catch up to them," Hugo yelled from the helm of the *panga* as they continued south past Bahia Santa Marta, Ensenada La Ballena, and then past Puerto Los Gatos to Timbabiche.

Hugo slowed the *panga* and pointing at the shore and said, "See that old house there just off the beach? That house has quite a story to it. There was a fisherman about fifty years ago that was so poor he didn't even have a boat. He fished from shore and harvested oysters by wading in the bay at low tide. One day he found an oyster with a very large, perfectly formed pearl in it. The pearl was reported to be almost ten millimeters in diameter. He sold the pearl for a relatively cheap price compared to its value," Hugo continued while they looked at the solitary, run down remnants of a large two-story home standing alone in the desert.

"The fortunate fisherman bought a fleet of *panga* fishing boats and built that house, called Casa Grande. He lived in that house with his family until he died of old age. The children did not want the house because it was so remote and far from any village, so they just let it go to ruin as you can see it now."

Later as they passed Punta Salinas, Hugo stated, "See those ruins on the shore? That is what is left of a large salt mining operation. It is like a ghost town now."

The abandoned buildings, rusting machinery and old vehicles were left to disintegrate in the sun and salt air.

"It would be fun to go ashore and explore this area. Maybe next time," Snake suggested.

About thirty minutes later, as they were passing a small, remote fishing village called Napolo, Hugo reported, "There is a sailboat ahead of us. That could be Just Dandy."

As they got closer, they could make out "Just Dandy" painted on the hull near the stern.

"Ahoy the sailboat," Snake yelled as they approached Just Dandy.

"Ahoy yourself," Annie yelled back with a smile on her face.

"Is everything OK?" Hugo asked as they got closer.

"All is well," Lola responded from the helm of Just Dandy.

"OK then, see you at San Evaristo," Hugo shouted as he moved the *panga* away to a southern heading and increased speed.

Hugo, Marty and Snake arrived at San Evaristo a few minutes later and entered the bay slowly. SV Hannah was the only boat in the remote bay and there was no activity at the shore as far as Snake could see through the field glasses.

"I can see three people in the cockpit of SV Hannah. Looks like Joe, Buck and Captain Kirk," Snake announced as they approached.

Captain Hugo placed three inflatable fenders on the starboard side of the *panga* and tossed a line to Captain Kirk who tied the *panga* to the port side of SV Hannah.

"Welcome aboard," Captain Kirk said as the three men climbed out of the *panga* and onto SV Hannah. Joe and Buck came up to Hannah's cockpit to greet them.

"How's it going you guys?" Joe greeted the trio.

"As well as can be expected. We passed Annie and Lola on Just Dandy. They should arrive here within the hour," Marty declared.

"How did you and Buck get here?" Marty asked Joe.

"We hired a *panguero* to bring us from La Paz. He dropped us off and left," Joe responded.

"I am expecting two more people to join us. After Annie and Lola arrive, I will explain," Marty said.

"I will make us a light lunch while we wait," Captain Kirk mentioned as he headed down to the galley.

A few minutes later the team was enjoying their toasted tuna sandwiches, homemade clam chowder and iced sun tea.

"Here comes JD now," Joe said as Just Dandy rounded the point.

After dropping her mainsail Just Dandy, began motoring into the bay at San Evaristo.

"You are just in time for lunch," Captain Kirk said as Annie tossed a line to him.

"Request permission to come aboard," Lola asked, after tying Just Dandy to Hannah's port side.

"Welcome aboard you two. If you go below and find a seat at the table in the salon, I will serve some lunch," Captain Kirk responded.

"That would be nice, thanks Kirk," Annie answered as the two women boarded Hannah.

Annie and Lola went below and found Joe, Marty, Snake, Buck and Hugo already seated at the large salon table.

"Welcome. Please take a seat and make yourselves comfortable," Joe said while Kirk prepared lunch in the galley for Lola and Annie.

"We understand Nicky has asked to meet Lola in four days at Ensenada de Los Muertos. Have you heard any more from Nicky since?" Joe asked.

"No, we have not heard any more from him, so we believe the meet is still scheduled. Nicky implied he would provide a doctor for an abortion when he meets Lola at Muertos. We think there is a good chance Nicky plans to kill Lola instead of providing an abortion," Annie continued.

"How do you feel about meeting with Nicky?" Joe asked Lola while the rest of the team listened.

"He is a bad man, and he needs to be stopped so he doesn't hurt any more people. I know Nicky is dangerous, but I trust you will protect me," Lola remarked as she looked at the other team members.

"We appreciate your trust in us," Joe responded as the

other team members nodded in agreement.

"There are some other issues we need to consider before we make a plan to take Nicky into custody. Marty was contacted by his superiors recently and asked to coordinate our plans to arrest Nicky with the help of two other US Government agencies who are also engaged in some especially important missions here on the Baja," Joe reported. "Marty, would you bring us up to speed with what you know about the other agencies and their missions?"

"Yes, of course. An assistant director contacted me directly via the STU phone and explained the Drug Enforcement Administration is engaged in an investigation involving several million dollars' worth of illegal drugs coming up from Columbia to the Baja, headed for the United States. I don't know much more than that about the drug investigation, but I am expecting a supervising agent from the DEA to arrive here today at San Evaristo to contact us and share some details."

"There is also another mission being conducted in our area by the Central Intelligence Agency, wouldn't you know," Marty said with a smile. "The only thing I've been told about the CIA operations is that their mission takes priority. A supervising CIA agent is also on his or her way here to work with us in coordinating our missions."

"Oh, I feel a headache coming on," Buck complained.

"You've got to be kidding," Annie responded.

"Let's wait to make any assumptions until after we hear from these folks," Joe suggested.

"What can go wrong, will go wrong. Murphy's law you call it. In México we call it Mungia's law," Hugo responded with a grin.

The sound of a loud aircraft motor heard passing over the bay caused everyone to go up on deck to see what was making the noise. A large single engine aircraft was about 300 feet above the water and turning to take another pass around the perimeter of the bay. The motor on the aircraft was unmuffled and loud as it passed overhead. It turned into a breeze from the north and then dropped down and landed on the calm water in the bay. It then motored over in the direction of SV Hannah.

"I will go out to meet it in the *panga*. Anyone want to help?" Hugo asked as he jumped in the *panga* and began untying it from SV Hannah.

"I will help," Annie offered as she climbed aboard the *panga* with Hugo.

The team watched from the cockpit and deck of Hannah as a man and a woman got out of the aircraft and stood on the plane's float while Hugo and Annie approached in the *panga*. The four people spoke to each other for a couple of minutes, then the woman opened the door to the aircraft and said something to the pilot. The man, carrying two bags, and the woman, carrying a briefcase, got into the *panga* with Hugo and Annie, and as the *panga* moved away from the aircraft, the pilot started its motor.

"That is a de Havilland Beaver, short takeoff and landing aircraft. It has a nine-cylinder radial motor that puts out 450 horsepower and has been called the best of all Alaskan bush planes," Buck said to no one in particular as Hugo, Annie and the two visitors slowly approached Hannah.

"Welcome aboard," Captain Kirk greeted the visitors.

"Let's gather in the salon around the table so we can be properly introduced," Joe suggested.

In the salon, after everyone took seats Joe began, "Why don't we start off by all of us introducing our team to our visitors. The two of you can then tell us who you are and what you have planned. Does that sound OK?" Joe asked.

"I'm Annie Diaz an FBI field agent, pilot and I speak Spanish," Annie said as she turned and looked at Marty.

"I'm Marty Goodson, supervising field agent with the FBI."

"I'm Captain Hugo Chávez with the Armada de México."

"I go by my nickname, Snake. I am retired from the US Army

as a Ranger and have been recalled to duty for this mission."

"I'm Buck Buchanan, FBI pilot."

"I'm Lola Flores."

"I'm Kirk Christian, skipper of Sailing Vessel Hannah. I've been contracted for the use of my sailboat."

"I'm Joe Creed, former police officer and now on leave as an insurance fraud investigator."

Please tell us who you are and what your mission is," Joe requested.

"Our names and our missions are classified secret, and we are not allowed to discuss anything with anyone who does not hold a secret clearance with the US government," the woman responded.

"Does anyone here have a current secret clearance?" the man asked.

No one responded and there was a long pause.

"I used to. Why did you come to visit us then?" Snake asked.

"We are here to ask you to terminate your mission in deference to our activities," the woman responded.

"What if we refuse?" Joe asked.

"Then we will need to proceed and deal with your interference as our mission dictates," the woman answered.

"Let me tell everyone what I learned from my superiors regarding the DEA and the CIA missions here on the Baja and maybe that will answer your questions," Marty interjected as the tension in the salon began to rise.

"As I understand it, a drug runner by the name of Pablo Escobar has leased a tramp steamer to haul fertilizer from Chile north to the Baja for a farming cooperative. Along with the fertilizer, Pablo has managed to include a large shipment of cocaine hidden aboard, destined ultimately for the US illegal drug market. Along with the fertilizer and cocaine, there are supposed to be three outdated Soviet nuclear artillery shells. The shells can produce a 1 kiloton nuclear blast and do not need to be fired from an artillery weapon since they can be detonated as an improvised explosive device or IED," Marty explained.

"You have revealed secret information to non-qualified individuals," the man stated.

"According to 10 US Code 1564 secret security information may be provided to qualified individuals in exigent circumstances provided they take an oath of secrecy," Marty reponded while pulling a thick publication from his bag.

"Let me look it up in the federal government policies and procedures manual. Yes, here it is. Look for yourself," Marty said as he handed the manual to the man.

After a few moments the man and woman looked over the code and whispered back and forth to each other.

The woman then said, "We can accept this and share our information but only if everyone here takes an oath and signs a document promising secrecy."

"Does anyone object to taking an oath of secrecy?" Joe asked.

"Do you have a typewriter?" the man asked, looking at Kirk.

Captain Kirk set up the typewriter with paper on the chart table of the sailboat and invited the man to take a seat. He typed and then read a document, which said:

"I will not disclose, communicate or convey or allow to be disclosed, communicated, or conveyed directly or indirectly to any person, group or agency, any secret, private or confidential information whatsoever obtained by me or in or about the performance of my duties or by virtue of my position with the group known as the US Government Baja Task Force; and I further promise and swear that I will not allow any person or persons to inspect or have access to any written statement, record, roll, return, correspondence, plan, photograph or any other paper or article over which I have any control and I will conscientiously endeavor to prevent any person from inspecting or having access to any such information as aforesaid.

Whatever I see or hear of a confidential or secret nature or that is confided to me in my official capacity will be kept ever secret unless revelation is necessary in the performance of my duties.

I shall not remove any written document from the Baja Task Force without the written consent of the Central Intelligence Agency or a designee.

"Do I need to sign this?" Captain Kirk asked.

"It's up to you, Kirk. If you want to know the details of our mission you need to take the oath," Joe said.

"If you don't want to take the oath then you will need to exclude yourself from our discussions," the man remarked.

"I suppose I should know what all of you are up to. OK, where do I sign?" Kirk asked with the pen in his hand.

After everyone signed the document, the woman stated, "Now since that is done, let me introduce myself to you. I am Donna Elaine Ashford, and I am a supervising agent with the United States Drug Enforcement Administration. We have been watching a drug runner named Pablo Escobar for some time and we found out he has completed a straw lease on a merchant vessel to carry 250 tons of ammonium nitrate fertilizer from Chile to a Guaymas, Sonora, México agriculture cooperative. The steamer drifted off the Pacific coast of Columbia for a couple hours on its way north while two *pangas* came out from the town of Buenaventura loaded to the brim with kilos of cocaine. They loaded the cocaine on board a recommissioned WWII Liberty ship named 'Bass Reeves' which then continued north. We expect it will enter the Sea of Cortez in ten days. We were planning a raid on the ship and the arrest of Pablo Escobar when we were contacted by the CIA. I will let Casey take it from here," Donna concluded while turning to the CIA agent.

"Good afternoon. I am Casey Igor Abbott, and I am a supervising case agent with the United States Central

Intelligence Agency, or 'agency' for short. The agency has been monitoring the movement of five nuclear 240-millimeter artillery shells from the Soviet Union that were sold to a European arms dealer recently. Each shell carries a one megaton nuclear capability and they do not need to be fired from an artillery gun to explode. They can be wired together as an improvised explosive device, or IED, and exploded with a timer or remotely with a radio signal. Three 240-millimeter nuclear artillery shells were loaded aboard Merchant Vessel Bass Reeves along with the cocaine. Pablo Escobar already has two 240-millimeter nuclear artillery shells which were delivered to him here in México about a month ago. We want to intercept those three nuclear weapons, arrest Pablo Escobar, and recover the remaining two artillery shells he has stored at his compound near San Javier. This mission takes priority over the missions of the DEA and the FBI," Casey declared.

There was a long silence as everyone pondered the seriousness of the circumstances just presented to them. Snake's tongue flicked in and out slightly between his lips as he stared intently at Casey.

"Well, it is clear to me we have to combine forces to intercept the nuclear weapons headed this way and to take custody of the weapons at Escobar's compound," Joe said.

"Nothing says we can't confiscate the cocaine at the same time and complete the DEA's mission," Donna remarked.

"If Nicky happens to be around, there is nothing that says we can't snatch his ass up either," Snake said.

"Yes, I think that is reasonable as long as we do not lose focus on the nukes," Joe agreed.

"With so many agencies represented and with so many ranks and commissions held by this group of law enforcement officers I would say the next task is to determine leadership roles so we can be efficiently organized and operate as a team," Marty suggested.

"Since the overriding mission is tasked with the agency, I propose that I take command of this combined task force," Casey announced.

"That sounds reasonable, except…," Marty paused.

"Except what?" Donna asked.

"Except the only person in this combined task force that has unfettered powers of arrest in México is Joe Creed. Captain Hugo Chávez of the Armada de México has arrest authority only in his district, which does not include our current location or anywhere, except the Loreto area on the Baja," Marty continued.

"Does the Mexican government have any knowledge that the DEA and CIA are engaged in clandestine operations in their country?" Marty asked.

"Absolutely not," Casey responded.

"I think I've made the case for Joe Creed to lead this mission unless anyone has an objection," Marty stated.

"I just want to make sure the agency's mission will be completed. How does a former foot patrolman from a small city come up with an arrest commission from the Mexican government?" Casey asked.

"I now work for a large multi-national insurance company that does a lot of business in México, Central and South America. My job is to review insurance claims that are suspicious or 'red flagged'. Part of my work is to manage and lead a team of Mexican investigators located in different areas throughout México and, because insurance fraud is a continuing problem in México, the CEO of my company asked the president of México to issue powers of arrest to the company's Mexican insurance investigators, including me," Joe reported. "The arrest commissions are not restricted and are authorized anywhere in México."

"So, even though our mission has nothing to do with insurance, you believe the Mexican government will support you in any arrest you make?" Casey asked.

"I wouldn't say our mission has nothing to do with insurance. Can you imagine the claims resulting from a nuclear explosion? To answer your question about the Mexican government supporting any arrest I make, let me say that I make no predictions what any politician of any country may do at any time. Leading this mission is going to be a large responsibility. I will accept it only if I can get a word of acceptance and confidence from every team member," Joe stated as he stood up.

"I have known you for a long time, Joe, and we have counted on each other in life and death situations so many times I can't count them. Let me be the first to say you have my full support," Marty said as he stood and shook Joe's hand.

The rest of the team lined up to shake Joe's hand and express their support.

"It has been my honor to work with you in Yakima, Joe. You have my full support," Snake stated as he shook Joe's hand.

They all shook Joe's hand and pledged their support.

Casey, however, stood up and said, "I'm still not comfortable with you leading this group. Since this mission was given to me, I consider it my responsibility."

"Casey, I have great respect for what you just said. I hope that you, Donna, or any other member of our team will support and share with me your knowledge, details and implications of a plan of action we develop," Joe commented.

"You have my tentative support, Joe, but I want to be included in every step of the mission," Casey responded.

"You have my promise on that," Joe responded as they shook hands.

"That calls for a cold drink and some snacks before supper. Lola caught three nice Dorado this morning from the stern of her sailboat, and she has dressed them out, and I will barbeque them for supper," Kirk explained as the team headed up through the companionway to the cockpit.

"Let's all meet in the cockpit after supper," Joe requested

as he joined the others.

"The captain asked me to take this up to you," Casey said as he climbed the companionway and handed a heavy cooler to Joe.

"OK, it must be important if the captain sent it. Let's look inside," Joe said as he placed the cooler on the deck and opened it. "Soda pop, iced tea, diet cola, beer and water," Joe said as he handed out drinks to the team.

"Thanks, Casey and Joe," Annie responded along with the rest of the team.

After a supper of barbequed Dorado, baked potato, corn on the cob and a salad with avocado, the team took a relaxing break while Joe reviewed in his mind the missions and plans of action facing them.

"Where do you get fresh corn on the cob and fresh avocado's during the winter, Kirk?" Donna asked.

"México has some nice winter crops of corn, avocado and many other vegetables. I stocked this boat full of provisions before we sailed and I'm glad I did now with ten people, including myself aboard," Kirk responded.

"Where is everybody going to sleep tonight?" Donna asked.

"I have 2 staterooms plus the captain's suite. There are two berths in each of my 2 staterooms, plus the two settees in the salon make into beds. Lola has room for four more, if necessary, aboard Just Dandy. Lola and Annie have their gear on Just Dandy. Donna, you might be more comfortable aboard the lady's boat, and I think she has plenty of water for showers. We seven guys on this 63-foot sailboat should be just fine," Kirk stated.

"Thanks, Kirk, I will check with Lola to see if I can move aboard Just Dandy for the night," Donna responded.

"Let's plan on a team meeting on Hannah in the salon after breakfast," Joe suggested as they bid each other good night.

12.

THE STRATAGEM

The next morning Kirk and Joe traded off kitchen duties in Hannah's galley, first getting coffee to everyone. Buck handed over cups of hot coffee to Annie, Lola and Donna in Just Dandy's cockpit. Just Dandy had spent the night tied to Hannah's port side, protected by several fenders, as Hannah was securely anchored to the sandy bottom in the peaceful bay.

Hashbrowns, sausage, and eggs with toast was served to the crew who took little time to finish their breakfasts. While Marty and Kirk finished cleaning up the galley the rest of the crew gathered around the large table in the Hannah's salon.

"I'm sure glad we are able to use your boat, Kirk. I'd hate to see us trying to get together on a smaller vessel," Joe mentioned.

"Well to get started, I would say that we have 3 main goals as a group. First in priority is to intercept and take custody of three nuclear artillery shells coming in this direction on MV Bass Reeves. Second, is to take custody of and confiscate a large shipment of cocaine also aboard MV Bass Reeves. It's due to arrive at the entrance of the Sea of Cortez in about 9 days. Finally, we want to arrest a very dangerous wanted felon who has promised to make contact with Lola in 3 days. Is there anything more to ad?" Joe asked.

"Casey, can you provide us with more information? What does Pablo Escobar plan to do with the nukes?" Marty asked.

"The agency thought the nukes were going to stay in Columbia and most analysts believed Pablo was going to use them to extort his government into appointing him president. He has been campaigning to be president of Columbia for some time now. When the first 2 nukes went north to Pablo's compound on the Baja, we became very concerned. The closer these nukes get to the United States border, the more worried everyone gets. Since 3 more nukes are being shipped north, the agency believes it is critical we act," Casey explained.

"What do these nuclear artillery shells look like?" Snake asked.

"Like any other artillery shell which looks like a huge bullet made out of steel. They are about 860 millimeters or about 34 inches long and 180 millimeters or about 7 inches in diameter. Each weighs just over 150 pounds and they are not dangerously radioactive in their current state," Casey explained.

"Does your agency have a plan to recover the nukes from MV Bass Reeves?" Joe asked.

"Yes, we have a squad of US Navy personnel ready to go at a moment's notice with a plan to board and take command of the ship. We believe it is safer to seize the ship and its contents while out to sea rather than in port. The assault team is ready to go at my command," Casey continued.

"What is your plan for the two nuclear artillery shells at Pablo's San Javier compound?" Annie asked.

"The nukes at Pablo's compound near Loreto are a separate mission which has been assigned to another assault team, which will also act on my command. Both teams have been practicing their raids and they are ready to go," Casey explained.

"Have you or any of your superiors notified the Mexican government of your plans?" Hugo asked.

"No, and we did not plan to notify your government of

any of this information," Casey answered.

"Don't you think it is a violation to invade another country by force, putting citizens at risk, without prior permission from the government of that sovereign country?" Hugo asked as his face began getting red.

"It may be, but we do it all the time," Casey responded.

"Wait a minute," Joe exclaimed, jumping into the conversation. "Hugo has a point, Casey. It seems awfully arrogant of you and your agency to just assume you can carry on an operation like this without approval or even notice to the Mexican government. How would you feel if México entered the United States with armed soldiers to carry out a military mission where there will most probably be collateral damage, without notice?" Joe asked.

"I don't want to have to go into the details of why we don't trust the Mexican government," Casey responded, looking Hugo in the eye.

"Your government is clean as a whistle?" Hugo asked sarcastically.

"Casey, let me ask you a question. Do you trust Hugo?" Marty asked as he stepped forward.

Everything was quiet for a moment.

"Yes, I trust Hugo. But I'm not sure about the people he may trust."

"Hugo, do you believe Casey will be honest with you?" Marty asked.

"Trust, but verify," Hugo responded with a smile.

"Why don't we lower our blood pressures a little by continuing our discussion over lunch," Captain Kirk stated from the galley.

"Maybe a shot of tequila would help too," Buck added with a grin.

A nervous chuckle emanated from the group as they gathered for lunch.

"Donna, can you tell us what your plans are regarding

the raid and seizure of the drugs?" Joe asked as they started lunch.

"The DEA and the CIA are linked together on this mission. Confiscation and/or destruction of the drugs are included in the overall mission," Donna explained.

"Let me share the proposed CIA and DEA joint mission details with everyone here," Casey declared. "Please remember this information is classified as secret and the release of any part of what I am about to tell you could get a number of people killed. Like I explained earlier, we have 2 teams of former US Navy underwater demolition divers that are specifically trained in commando and counter guerrilla warfare. Their training includes clandestine operations in maritime environments, hand to hand combat, high altitude parachuting and demolitions. They call themselves Navy SEALs. They were established in 1961 at the direction of Admiral Arleigh Burke, with the approval of President Kennedy, out of a need evolving from the Korean and Vietnam Wars."

"The SEALs will approach MV Bass Reeves under the cover of darkness after the vessel has entered into shallow water, but still away from shore and other vessels. This will reduce the chance of collateral damage. There are parts of the Sea of Cortez that are nearly 2 miles deep. We do not want Bass Reeves to disappear beyond our reach if something goes wrong and we are not able to seize the nukes before she sinks," Casey continued.

"There are a number of rivers that flow into the Sea of Cortez from the Mexican mainland that cause many of the areas directly off the west coast of the Mexican mainland to be shallow. The center of the Sea of Cortez is where the depths are the greatest, so, it depends on the route Bass Reeves takes, and the stage of the moon during her nighttime travels, as to when we make our move on the vessel. The second SEAL team will assault the San Javier compound at the same time we move on Bass Reeves. It appears we have plenty of time before we act," Casey explained.

"Are you able to track Bass Reeves movements in real time?" Joe asked.

"Yes, don't ask me how, but the agency knows exactly where that ship is, its speed and direction at any moment in time," Casey responded.

"Are you able to stay in close contact with your agency from here on the Baja?" Snake asked.

"No, it has been difficult keeping in contact and we need to establish a secure contact method as soon as possible," Casey responded.

"We have an FBI, STU phone hooked up at the naval base at Puerto Escondido that I'm sure you can use," Hugo advised.

"What do all of you think about Casey, Donna, Hugo and Buck heading back to Puerto Escondido in the *panga* to establish contact with Casey's office, so that we can keep track of Bass Reeves and make our move when the time is right?" Joe asked the team.

"We may need the use of the director's jet aircraft or some armaments as these missions proceed, Buck," Joe remarked.

"Good thought Joe, I will keep the Gulfstream II ready to go at a moment's notice," Buck responded.

"Will we be able to keep in contact with you from Ensenada de los Muertos to Puerto Escondido?" Donna asked.

"It is too far for the VHF and the FBI portable scrambled radios, but I can easily pick up a ham radio signal, just give me the frequency," Kirk said.

The group worked out the details and made preparations for Captain Hugo to take DEA agent Donna Ashford, CIA agent Casey Abbott, and FBI Pilot Buck Buchanan in the *panga* back north to Puerto Escondido in the morning.

"Our next task is to make a plan on how to capture Nicolas James Cabot when he meets Lola the day after tomorrow at Muertos Bay," Joe remarked.

13.

EL DIABLO

" **I** brought these items from the armory on board the directors jet aircraft," Joe reported as he placed two strange looking pistols on the table in Hannah's cockpit.

"What do you have there?" Snake asked.

"This one is called an electric pistol. It is a non-lethal prototype, recently invented. The other pistol is a simple .50 caliber tranquilizer gun. We can use either or both, if necessary, for this mission to capture Nicky alive," Joe remarked.

"I think I read something from the FBI academy recently about the electric pistol, but how does it actually work?" Annie asked.

"I can give you a quick explanation before we leave, since I've received some training on all of the weapons in the aircraft's armory, but I need two volunteers for a demonstration," Buck said.

"Maybe Lola should be instructed on how to use it since she may need it to help capture Nicky," Joe advised.

"Do you need a victim in this non-lethal demonstration?" Snake asked.

"Yes, Snake. We need someone to get shot by this electric gun to show how well it works," Buck responded.

"OK, I will volunteer to be the victim in this demo as

long as you guarantee it will be non-lethal. I would like to see how effective this thing is," Snake said with a smile.

Buck handed the electric pistol to Lola, and they took a position near the entrance to the companionway in the cockpit of Hannah while Snake stood back near the stern at a distance of about 12 feet.

"This is the safety mechanism, and it works like this. The sights and trigger work essentially the same as a regular revolver except after the pistol is fired, one needs to hold the trigger down to send a high voltage charge through the wires attached to the darts that are fired and stuck in the suspect's skin. When you let up on the trigger, after the darts are fired and stuck in the suspect's skin, the electric current stops until you pull the trigger again sending current down the wires to the darts, causing the suspect to be incapacitated," Buck explained.

"OK, let's do it. Sorry, Snake, I don't mean to hurt you," Lola said.

"Yes, you do. But I forgive you," Snake responded with a smile.

Pop! went the pistol, and immediately two darts, with thin wires attached, flew out of the barrel and stuck on Snake's chest. A buzzing sound ensued as the high voltage electricity raced through the thin wires and into Snake's body causing him to immediately convulse and fall to the deck.

"Oh God, I'm sorry, Snake," Lola said as she let up on the electric pistol's trigger and placed the gun on the table.

"Whew, that was fun!" Snake exclaimed as he began to get up.

Annie picked up the pistol that still had the darts and wires attached to Snake and pulled the trigger again. Snake immediately convulsed and dropped to the deck again as his eyes rolled back in his head. Annie, realizing what she had done, dropped the pistol which stopped the high voltage charge.

"Hey, it works well. We don't need to test it again," Snake

yelled as he tried to stand up.

"I am sorry, Snake I thought it was discharged," Annie said apologetically.

"It will have enough charge for about 10 shots. Let me show you how to reload it," Buck said as he pulled out the darts stuck in Snake's chest and rearmed the pistol.

"There was no way I could do anything after being shot and electrocuted by that pistol. It is a good non-lethal weapon," Snake reported.

"The tranquilizer gun shoots a dart filled with a solution of benzodiazepine which puts the suspect quickly to sleep. Care needs to be taken, however, in the event of an overdose. The suspects vital signs need to be monitored after use," Buck explained as he showed how the tranquilizer pistol operates and reloads.

"You don't need to demonstrate how that tranquilizer gun works do you?" Snake asked Buck.

"No, it is pretty simple. It only has a range of about 10 yards but works better the closer one is to the target. One should aim for the suspect's large muscle mass like a leg, buttocks, arm or shoulder," Buck instructed.

Captain Hugo, DEA Agent Donna Ashford, CIA Agent Casey Abbott, and FBI Pilot Buck Buchanan all boarded the *panga*. The lines were untied from Hannah and the *panga* slowly motored away with Captain Hugo at the helm. They turned north, increased speed, and headed back to the navy base at Puerto Escondido with the intent of following the approaching movements of the old Liberty Ship, MV Bass Reeves, which was loaded with fertilizer, 3 nuclear artillery shells, and a shipment of cocaine.

Meanwhile, Kirk raised Hannah's anchor and motored out of San Evaristo Bay heading south toward Ensenada de las Muertos, an 18-hour sail, while Lola and Annie followed in Just Dandy.

"Nicky told me to meet him in Ensenada de los Muertos. He said to leave Just Dandy's swim ladder down," Lola explained.

"I suspect he will show up after dark," Annie responded.

"Let's assume he climbs aboard Just Dandy using the swim ladder. How should we proceed with his capture when he arrives?" Annie asked.

"We don't want to be too close and spook him since he is expecting Lola to be alone," Marty said.

"But we don't want to be too far away unless Lola needs our help," Snake advised.

After arriving, Joe and Marty got into Hannah's inflatable dinghy and motored over to Just Dandy which was anchored about 400 yards away in the bay at Ensenada de los Muertos, while Kirk remained on Hannah. Lola tied the inflatable dinghy to the port side of Just Dandy, tied a fender horizontally from Just Dandy's rail to act as a step, opened the gate, and invited everyone aboard.

"What a delightful boat," Joe mentioned as he climbed aboard.

"She is 32 feet long, just over 10 feet wide with a draft of 6.5 feet. She carries 30 gallons of fresh water and 18 gallons of diesel fuel," Lola explained.

"Her cockpit is not large, but it is comfortable," Snake mentioned as he looked the boat over.

"There is stowage in the lazarette under the starboard side cockpit seat," Lola reported as she lifted the lid. "There is an additional deep stowage area under the seat in the stern on the port side," Lola continued as she made her way down the stairs of the companionway into the salon of the boat.

Annie, Snake, Marty, and Joe followed down inside the sailboat. Just Dandy had a well-appointed interior, dressed out in glossy, varnished teak wood covering the sole and cabinetry of the sailboat. There was a head which included a shower on the starboard side aft of the boat, and on the port side was the aft stateroom. The 3-cylinder, Universal, 24 horsepower diesel motor sat in the middle between the head and the aft stateroom under an insulated teak cover. Just forward of the head on the starboard side of the vessel was the chart table with an instrument panel including the switches necessary for 12 volt and 110-volt shore power. Mounted nearby were VHF, Ham and AM-FM radios. Opposite the chart table on the port side was the galley and a propane stove with two burners and a small oven, mounted on a gimble, which kept the stove level when out to sea. There were settees on both sides of the salon that made into sleeping berths. A foldable table attached to the mast in the middle between the settees was large enough when opened to be used as a small dining table and above it, just forward of the mast, was a large hatch with a clear plastic window that opened to the deck.

In the bow of the boat, separated from the salon by a curtain, was the V-berth. It was large enough to sleep two and also had a large hatch that opened to the deck at the bow of the vessel.

"I think Lola should be covered with at least two backups within arm's reach to protect her as much as possible. Nicky may have designs to kill her instead of providing a doctor for an abortion like he promised," Marty suggested.

"I can hide out in that deep stowage locker at the stern of the boat if someone else can cover Lola from the V-berth," Snake said.

"I can hide in the V-berth and even go on to the foredeck through the hatch, if necessary," Annie reported.

"Someone should be ashore near Just Dandy, and someone should be available to respond quickly on the water in the event things go in either direction," Joe mentioned.

"I can dig out my camos and take the shore duty," Marty volunteered.

"I guess that leaves me to remain aboard Hannah with her tender ready to go if we need to respond on the water," Joe said.

"We have our hand-held scrambled portable radios with earpieces. Let's all make sure we are on channel 22," Annie remarked.

"When Nicky climbs aboard you will feel the boat move. When that happens why don't we key the microphone 4 times without saying anything to alert everyone?" Snake suggested as everyone nodded in agreement.

"My guess is Nicky will swim to Just Dandy after dark, swim around and under her to quietly check things out and then climb slowly aboard on the stern ladder. The boat will move slightly as he climbs the ladder, but it will not move much. When he comes aboard, I will call out his name and try to hug him. Otherwise, I will say nothing until he arrives," Lola declared.

Just before dusk Marty and Joe untied Hannah's inflatable tender from Just Dandy and returned slowly to Hannah while Snake, Annie and Lola made preparations for Nicky's arrival. Snake put his flashlight, his .38-caliber pistol, a military bayonet knife, some jerky and water in a bag. He silently slipped into the dark aft stowage locker space in the stern of the sailboat and closed the lid.

Annie climbed onto the V-berth in the bow of the boat, pulled the curtain closed separating the sleeping quarters from the salon, and slightly opened the hatch in the low ceiling of the V-berth. She could see the shoreline through the partially opened hatch over the bow of the boat, which was facing north in the light breeze, while at anchor.

The wait began as the sun slowly dropped in the clear blue sky. As the temperature decreased, causing the land to cool quicker than the sea, the air movement stopped, and it became deadly calm. The sea was like glass and the palm trees ashore were standing silently quiet as the daylight diminished.

Marty swam ashore from Hannah with his camouflaged fatigues, weapons, radio, and gear in a waterproof knapsack. He dressed and armed himself in the bushes above the beach and then began quietly moving through the brush toward Just Dandy. Up off the beach, near Just Dandy, Marty dug a trench and placed brush around it. He then lay down in the trench where he could easily see Just Dandy. A mile down the beach, in front of the resort, some people were gathering and building a bonfire.

Joe tied Hannah's tender at her stern suggesting the occupants remained aboard the sailboat. She was quietly anchored about 400 yards west of Just Dandy in Ensenada de los Muertos, or in English, The Bay of the Dead.

Lola took a long drink from a bottle of Hornitos Anejo Tequila. She then hid the electric pistol between the cushions on the settee and the tranquilizer gun in the rail on the starboard side, loosely wrapped in a towel, both within easy reach. Lola turned on the boat's anchor light and went up to the cockpit and turned on a light over the table. Everyone waited quietly, listening on channel 22 and watching for Nicky's arrival.

There was little ambient light in Muertos, a yard light at the restaurant on the northeast shore, and one other light about a mile southwest at a small resort. Both lights reflected off the water and there was a waning gibbous moon which also shined off the mirrorlike surface of the bay. The sound of a whale blowing came from outside the bay in the quiet air of dusk, and the brightness of the Milky Way and other star formations began to stand out in the dry, cool air of the approaching evening. Ursa Major was tilted, pouring imaginary water from the ladle, and the North Star stood out like a beacon. The distant howl from a coyote was heard in the quiet air as everyone waited.

Then, something quietly bumped into the bow of the boat and the boat began to move, listing slightly to starboard. Annie looked out through the one-half inch opening in the hatch and saw a hand come up over the bow. It grabbed onto the railing near the anchor chain and began to climb aboard.

It was Nicky, he was climbing aboard at the bow instead of the swim ladder at the stern. Annie quickly keyed the transmit button four times on her portable radio, alerting the team that Nicky had arrived. Marty heard the four clicks in his earpiece and was surprised that Nicky had gotten past him without being seen.

I can see almost two miles of the beach in this bay and did not see Nicky enter the water. He must have approached in some other manner, Marty thought.

He then remembered how Nicky had escaped from Captain Hugo in the caves at Agua Verde using SCUBA gear, a battery powered SDV, and a *panga* hidden outside the bay.

Nicky was barefoot, wearing a dark shorty wetsuit, and the only weapon Annie could see was a diver's knife strapped to his right leg. Nicky silently made his way along the starboard side of the boat toward the stern where Lola was sitting in the cockpit.

"Hi, Lola," Nicky greeted as he poked his head around the dodger, smiling at Lola.

Snake heard the 4 clicks in his earpiece and was on alert while hiding in the stowage locker at the stern of the boat, now just a couple feet from Lola and Nicky.

"Nicky, I wish you wouldn't do that, you startled me," Lola responded with a smile on her face.

"*¿Como estas, mi amor?*" Lola asked.

"I'm OK except for all those US cops running around the Baja looking for me," Nicky responded.

"Let's go down inside. I made some of your favorite dessert, a nice flan," Lola suggested as she moved toward the companionway.

"Are you alone here?" Nicky asked.

"Of course, me amor, just you and me."

Annie moved quietly over to the corner, trying to be invisible in case Nicky moved aside the curtain and looked into the V-berth. Lola went to the galley and took out two small plates, forks and napkins while Nicky sat down on the starboard side settee. As Lola approached with the desert, Nicky stood up and said, "unfortunately, I don't have time for that."

"So, what is your plan, Nicky?"

"Come here, give me a hug," Nicky responded.

As the two embraced, Nicky cunningly reached down his right leg, removed the dagger from its sheath, and held the point just below Lola's belly button.

"This is my plan," Nicky said as he pushed the dagger into Lola's abdomen while looking deep into her eyes.

"Oooh," Lola quietly responded as the tip of the dagger found its way through her insides, to just short of her spine.

Nicky held her close while holding tightly onto his dagger. Lola could not get at the electric pistol, or the tranquilizer gun, and Snake and Annie had not yet realized what was happening. Lola was finally able to reach her right rear pocket in spite of her pain and shock. She took out the little .22 derringer firearm, cocked it and held the tip of the barrel against Nicky's forehead and fired as they continued to embrace. The bullet to Nicky's brain caused him to arch violently backward, while still tightly gripping the dagger. In one motion the knife opened Lola's mid-section with a cut that went from below her belly button to her heart. Both lovers immediately dropped like wilted flowers to the sole of the sailboat, while continuing to embrace.

Annie and Snake immediately responded to the gunshot, but there was nothing they could do. Snake scrambled out of his hiding place and Annie moved toward the couple, but it was too late. After being alerted, Marty and Joe quickly made their way to Just Dandy to find there was nothing anyone could do. Joe, Marty, Annie and Snake sat silently in Just Dandy's cockpit for several minutes contemplating what had just happened.

"Damn, how did this happen? We were supposed to protect her and now she's dead." Snake said while hanging his head.

"May her soul rest in peace. She was a courageous woman," Joe lamented.

"I knew something was wrong during their embrace, but I couldn't get to them," Annie said with tears in her eyes.

"What do we do now?" Snake asked.

"I think we should leave everything as undisturbed as possible so that Mexican law enforcement can process the scene," Marty suggested.

"We could take Just Dandy back to Puerto Escondido for Captain Hugo to request a formal murder investigation," Marty continued.

"The crime scene is on Just Dandy, and I see no problem moving her undisturbed to the navy base at Puerto Escondido," Joe asserted.

"We will have to move the bodies to get to the main switch for the diesel motor," Annie said.

"Let's leave everything as it is, tie a line to her bow, and have Hannah tow her to Puerto Escondido," Marty suggested.

"Before you raise her anchor, I'd like to check out the sandy bottom below Just Dandy. I'm wondering if Nicky left SCUBA gear on the bottom under Just Dandy since he was not seen entering the water anywhere near here," Joe explained.

"I was wondering the same thing. Let's look," Marty responded.

"What's that sound?" Snake asked as a soft clinking sound began emanating from Just Dandy's interior.

"*Ca-chink, Ca-chink, Ca-chink,* " went the sound in a slow, rhythmic pattern.

"That sound is the automatic bilge pump. It starts up on its own when water enters the bilge," Annie explained.

"Do you think Nicky punched a hole in the hull?" Joe asked.

"Are we sinking?" Snake asked.

"There must be water in the bilge. The question is, where is it coming from?" Annie asked.

"There are some tapered wooden plugs in a black plastic

bag under the sink in the galley if you can get to them," Annie continued.

"Look!" Annie exclaimed as she pointed to the water around the boat.

"It's red. It's blood. The boat is surrounded by bloody water!" Snake exclaimed.

"Where is it coming from?" Marty asked.

"The automatic bilge pumps are pumping Lola and Nicky's blood out of the bilge and into the sea," Annie finally explained.

"Oh, My God," Joe said, sitting down in the cockpit.

After a few minutes the automatic bilge pump stopped and the water around Just Dandy slowly cleared up. The former lover's blood merged and dissipated into the waters of the Sea of Cortez.

Joe and Marty retrieved their snorkeling gear from Hannah and returned to Just Dandy wearing short wetsuits, fins, masks, and snorkels for the dive to the bottom under Just Dandy.

Joe surfaced near the stern and said, "Annie, would you find me a line about fifty feet long in the lazarette and toss it to me?"

Joe dove to the bottom with the line and in a few moments he came to the surface with Marty. They handed one end of the line to Annie and Snake.

"We found SCUBA gear below. It's tied to the line, please pull it up," Marty explained.

Snake and Annie hauled the gear aboard Just Dandy and stowed it in the aft stowage compartment, where Snake had previously been hiding.

"There's more gear so we will need to use that rope again. By the way, I checked Just Dandy's hull from below and it all looks good," Marty reported.

A battery-powered swimmer delivery vehicle (SDV) was found on the bottom and hauled aboard and also stowed in the aft locker.

"I will take the dinghy over to Hannah and bring her anchor up. We can then tie a towline to Just Dandy and head back to Puerto Escondido," Joe declared.

"OK, we will get Just Dandy ready to go," Annie responded.

After Joe made his way over to Hannah, Kirk stated, "Let's get Hannah's dinghy up on the davits and raise the anchor so we can get under way. Watch for water coming out of the exhaust pipe," Kirk announced as he started the Hannah's diesel motor.

"Looks good," Joe responded.

Joe went to Hannah's bow and directed Kirk as he engaged the windlass to raise the anchor.

"She's secure," Joe reported after tying down Hannah's anchor to its cradle on the bow.

With Captain Kirk at the helm, Hannah slowly motored over to Just Dandy. Snake and Annie tied Just Dandy's tender to her stern to be towed, and Annie tossed a heavy dockline from the bow to Joe as Hannah motored close by. Joe tied the line to Hannah's stern cleat while Annie and Snake raised Just Dandy's anchor and locked her rudder at zero degrees. The two sailboats slowly left the bay with Hannah towing Just Dandy and her inflatable tender following. They turned north for the 140-mile, 29-hour trip to Puerto Escondido with Hannah's diesel motor running at 25 hundred RPM's, moving the boats at just over 5 knots per hour. As they rounded the north entrance to the bay, Kirk pointed out a lone *panga* on the beach by itself.

"I will bet that is Nicky's *panga*," Kirk said as he pointed to the boat.

"Let's check it out," Joe responded as Kirk reduced speed to 2 knots.

"I can hold here while you take the dinghy ashore and check it out," Kirk mentioned.

Joe lowered Hannah's dinghy to the water, started the

motor, went to Just Dandy and picked up Marty, then they headed for the beached *panga*. About 30 minutes later, after confirming it was Nicky's *panga*, Joe returned to Hannah in the dinghy with Marty following in the *panga*. Joe raised Hannah's dinghy back up on the davits and took the line from Nicky's *panga*. After Marty climbed aboard Hannah, they tied Nicky's *panga* to a cleat at Hannah's stern on the port side.

"We look like a parade with Nicky's *panga*, Just Dandy and her tender all tied to Hannah," Kirk commented.

"Is it too much for Hannah to tow everything?" Joe asked.

"It should be OK as long as we don't run into some bad weather or rough seas," Kirk responded.

"Do you see those red and green buoys off to the northeast?" Kirk asked Joe and Marty. "That is the San Lorenzo Channel. We need to go between those buoys to avoid grounding," Kirk explained.

"Do you want me to stay aboard Hannah, or should I return to Just Dandy?" Marty asked Kirk.

"Let's give them a call on VHF and see what they think," Kirk responded.

"Just Dandy, Just Dandy, Hannah," Marty repeated into the VHF radio microphone on channel 16.

"Go ahead, Hannah," Annie responded.

"Do the two of you feel comfortable enough standing watch as we continue to motor, or do you want me to return to Just Dandy?" Marty asked.

"We are good, but let's keep an open channel in case there's a challenge," Annie responded. "OK, we will continue to monitor channel 16, let us know if you need anything, Hannah out," Marty concluded.

"We seem to be making an average of 5 knots, which isn't too bad. How long do you think it will take to arrive at Puerto Escondido?" Joe asked.

"We should fetch Puerto Escondido about 29 hours if we can maintain 5 knots," Kirk responded.

"Which watch would you like to take?" Kirk asked Joe.

"I will take the first night watch if you like skipper."

"OK Joe, I have plotted a course on the chart table below. You might want to familiarize yourself with the navigational aids, compass headings and hazards indicated on the chart for the areas we will be sailing after dark."

Joe and Marty went down Hannah's companionway to the salon and looked over the chart with the course penciled north Captain Kirk laid out for them.

"I would love to check out Balandra Beach with Mushroom Rock just a few miles west of here," Joe said, looking at the chart.

"Yes, and just a few miles beyond Balandra is the pretty little city of La Paz. Did you like La Paz?" Marty asked.

"Yes, very much, the *malecón* follows the beach for several miles, and it is very clean and pleasant," Joe responded.

"They even have Seattle Seahawk games on TV at the Tailhunter Bar," Joe said with a smile.

The sun was getting low in the western sky, highlighting the red cliffs, the white sandy beaches and the dark green mangroves on Isla Espiritu Santo to the east. Hannah and her entourage passed by, continuing northbound, after making her way through the San Lorenzo Channel.

"Looks like a beach bonfire on Espiritu Santo," Joe reported, pointing east.

"That is Bahia San Gabriel on the island. It is a good place to set up a tent and do some camping," Kirk explained.

"Just Dandy, Just Dandy, Hannah," Kirk called into the VHF radio microphone.

"Just Dandy, go ahead, Hannah," Snakes voice responded over the radio.

"Go to channel 22," Kirk requested.

"OK, on channel 22."

"How is everything going?" Kirk asked.

"No problems so far on the death ship," Snake replied.

"I suggest you check the tow line to make sure it is not chaffing. You might also want to turn on your running lights since it will be dark soon," Kirk advised as he turned on Hannah's running and steaming lights.

"There is a sea lion colony just north of Isla Partida which is the next island that will appear off the starboard bow in a couple of hours. Just north of Isla Partida are some rocks with a flashing white navigation light. If it's not too dark, we might be able to see the sea lion colony," Kirk announced over the radio before signing off and going back to monitor channel 16.

The monotonous rumble of Hannah's small diesel motor continued as she maintained a compass heading of 315 degrees magnetic, with Just Dandy, the tender, and Nicky's *panga* in tow. The moon came out its waning glory, lighting up the sea and the islands off to the east as they continued north. The rocks north of Isla Partida were too far off to make out any members of the sea lion colony, but the flashing white navigation light confirmed Hannah's location on the chart.

"It is almost 10 PM Joe, I think I will go down inside and take a nap if you think you can manage this parade of boats without me for a couple of hours. There is a white light on Isla San Francisco that flashes once every 4 seconds and another directly across the Canal de San Jose at Cabeza de Mechudo. Steer a course directly between them, Joe, and there won't be any problems. Just beyond Isla San Francisco are some rocks called Rocas de la Foca. There is a white light that flashes twice every 10 seconds on the rocks. The next light to the port side will be at San Evaristo which flashes white 3 times every four seconds. From San Evaristo it is only 44 miles to Agua Verde and then just 21 more miles to Puerto Escondido," Kirk explained.

"I will keep an eye on things too, Captain. I wonder where the old Liberty Ship Bass Reeves is about now?" Marty asked.

"It should still be way south of here," Joe responded.

"I guess we will find out when we get back to the navy base at Puerto Escondido," Marty remarked.

SV Hannah, with vessels in tow, continued north through the night, past Isla San Francisco and Isla San Jose and the light at San Evaristo, on the Baja Peninsula. They approached Agua Verde just after sunrise and were continuing north past the small fishing village when a *panga* was observed heading out towards them from shore.

"Just Dandy, Just Dandy, Hannah," Joe called over the VHF radio.

"Go ahead, Hannah," Annie responded.

"Go to channel 22, Just Dandy," Joe stated.

"OK on 22 – what's up?"

"Be advised, we have a *panga* coming this way from the bay at Agua Verde," Joe said.

"OK, thanks, we will keep an eye on it," Annie replied.

The *panga* contained one male adult and it swiftly approached Just Dandy, pulled up and motored slowly alongside as the man in the *panga* spoke Spanish with Annie. He then left, and headed back to Agua Verde at full speed.

"What was that about?" Marty asked over the radio.

"That was Enrique, Leona's husband. She has the beach restaurant at Agua Verde. He wanted to know why we were towing Lola's boat and where Lola was," Annie explained.

"What did you tell him?" Marty asked.

"I told him we were taking Lola's boat to the navy base at Puerto Escondido and that I could not say more about Lola until after we made contact with her family first," Annie explained.

"I think he understood. Then he left," Annie remarked.

Joe pointed to the beach at Agua Verde and said to Marty, "Take a look at that."

"We have about 8 *pangas* leaving the beach at Agua Verde, all headed this way," Marty announced over the radio.

After a few minutes 9 *pangas*, loaded with people fell in behind and beside Just Dandy. One panga approached and a woman spoke to Annie and then sat back down with her head in her hands, crying. The 9 *pangas* followed along with Hannah in the lead, all headed to Puerto Escondido. They all arrived at the south entrance to Puerto Escondido in 5 hours and motored sadly and quietly into the bay, tying to the dock at the navy facility.

Joe, Marty, Annie, Kirk, and Snake all greeted the people from Agua Verde on the dock and offered their condolences.

"She was not a perfect person, but she was one of ours," Leona declared.

"She was a woman of great courage and honor," Snake said to the group with Annie interpreting. "Lola is responsible for stopping this vile, former police detective from causing harm to anyone else, and she should be recognized for her courage," Snake continued.

"Lola was critical in this mission. Nicky Cabot would still be a threat to the lives of many Mexican and US citizens if he had not been stopped. He would still be causing harm if it were not for Lola Flores who gave her life to protect others. She is a hero in my opinion, and I will be submitting an application to my superiors to formally recognize her courage," Marty reported to Lola's friends and family with Annie again interpreting.

Captain Hugo Chávez and two armed sailors approached and made contact with Marty and Joe. Hugo looked Just Dandy over and then posted the two sailors to secure the sailboat and not allow anyone aboard until further notice.

"I will contact my superiors and a navy investigative team to process this scene. Meanwhile please make yourselves comfortable and available to answer questions the investigators may have of you," Hugo stated to the team.

Captain Hugo also invited Lola's friends and relatives to the lounge and cafeteria at the navy base if they wished, before returning to Agua Verde.

"Lola's remains will be released to the family after the autopsy which may take a few days. Nicky's body will be sent to a mortuary in Loreto after the autopsy. When the scene has been processed relatives can claim him," Hugo advised.

"How are things going with MV Bass Reeves?" Marty quietly asked Hugo.

"Bass Reeves is headed this way and should approach Puerto Escondido in about 2 days if she maintains on her current heading and speed," Hugo responded.

"How are CIA and DEA doing?" Marty asked with Joe listening.

"They are like Iguanas on a hot tile roof," Hugo responded with a smile.

"We should go talk to them to see if there is anything we can do to help," Joe suggested with Marty nodding in agreement as they excused themselves from the gathering.

"I am really happy with the way our two agencies are working with each other for the same goal. It is good you have stopped Nicolas Cabot. Now we need to go after Pablo Escobar and keep him from using nuclear weapons to destroy our countries," Hugo advised.

As Hugo, Joe and Marty were walking to Hugo's office Lieutenant Veronica approached and saluted Captain Hugo and asked, "*¿Puedes decirme dónde está la serpiente buena, Capitán?*"

"She wants to know where the 'good serpent' might be," Hugo translated.

"Snake is on the dock with the people from Agua Verde," Joe responded with a smile.

"A romance in the making," Hugo mentioned with a grin as they continued walking to Hugo's office.

"On January 15, 1951, Santa Rosalia Police Chief Parra Rodriguez disarmed and arrested a serial killer from the United States named Billy Cook, without incident. Billy had been holding two hostages at gunpoint in a Santa Rosalia restaurant. The murderer was later taken to the border and turned over to US authorities. We need more cooperation like that between our two countries," Hugo explained.

"I agree and I appreciate how we have been trusted and treated by you and your country," Marty remarked.

Later Casey Abbot, CIA agent, was talking on the STU phone when Joe, Marty and Hugo returned to Hugo's office. Donna Ashford, DEA agent, was listening to the conversation on a speaker phone and taking notes. The men quietly took seats and waited until Casey had finished.

"Welcome back gentlemen. I heard you were very successful in your mission to take Nicolas Cabot into custody," Casey stated while rising from his chair.

"Yes, we got Nicky alright, but I would not characterize our completed mission as 'very successful' since we lost a brave soul," Joe responded.

"Yes, sorry to hear about that," Donna said with Casey nodding in agreement.

"How are things going with Bass Reeves?" Marty asked.

"Bass Reeves is about 2 days south of Puerto Escondido, still moving at about 5 knots northbound according to an update we just received. Our plan is to wait until Bass Reeves arrives closer to Puerto Escondido, at which time I expect to give a green light to the two SEAL teams to assault MV Bass Reeves and Pablo's compound at San Javier at the same time," Casey reported.

"Have any other vessels made contact with the ship as she motors north?" Joe asked.

"That is a good question. It appears she has been steaming steadily northbound and has had no contacts with other vessels as far as we can tell," Casey answered.

"Where are your SEAL teams staging," Joe asked.

"At the Mexican Military Airstrip at San Lucas, just south of Santa Rosalia, on the Baja Peninsula," Donna responded.

"What is the weather forecast two days from now?" Marty asked.

"Clear, with a 5 to 10 knot breeze out of the northwest, and the moon in its last quarter," Donna continued.

"It looks like everything is in place for a good outcome," Casey remarked.

"Anything else to report?" Hugo asked.

"There is one thing that concerns us. It appears someone else is monitoring MV Bass Reeves movements. One of our high-flying surveillance aircraft has spotted what appears to be other aircraft following the ship. We tried to identify the aircraft but were unable to do so," Casey explained.

"What did they look like?" Joe asked.

"There were two small, brightly lit aircraft that rotated counterclockwise about one thousand feet above the ship on several occasions," Donna explained.

"What do you mean brightly lit?" Joe asked.

"Bright balls of light," Donna responded.

14.

THE LIGHTS OF LORETO

S nake entered the room and whispered something to Joe. "Lola's friends and relatives are about to return to Agua Verde, and I want to see them off," Joe said.

Joe, Marty and Hugo walked together to the dock to again offer condolences.

"Balls of light," Joe remarked to Marty as they walked.

"Yea, figure that one out. It sounds like the same thing we saw on the airplane and again over Pablo Escobar's compound," Marty responded.

"Maybe we should go to Loreto and contact Padre Papa and see if there has been any more activity," Joe suggested.

"I would sure like to know what those lights are about. Maybe we can touch base with Buck and the guys at the airport on our way to town," Marty responded.

"Yes, and maybe we can visit Domingo's Steak House, too. I'd bet Annie would like to unwind a little," Joe said.

"Great idea. Why don't you see if she would like to go while I ask Hugo if he has a vehicle we can use to get to town," Marty suggested.

"Here are the keys to a Mexican Navy Ford van and a pass with my signature if anyone inquires why two gringos are driving a navy vehicle," Hugo mentioned to Marty, Joe and Annie as he handed them the keys with a smile.

"Thanks, Hugo. We should be back before dark," Joe responded.

The drive to the airport took about 15 minutes and upon arrival they found FBI Agents Hank Carter, Jack Rosen, and pilot Buck Buchanan in lawn chairs in the shade of the starboard wing of the director's aircraft. A picnic table, BBQ grill and cooler were nearby.

"Are we in time for lunch?" Marty asked as they approached.

"Could be. Jack has been eyeing that rooster over near the fence," Buck responded as he stood to shake hands.

After the team caught up on recent events with each other over refreshments, they all climbed into the van for a trip to Domingo's Restaurant, except for Marty, who remained to watch over the aircraft.

"I'm going to get the biggest steak they have on the menu," Hank announced during the trip to Domingo's.

"I might even order two steaks," Jack responded with a laugh.

After a satisfying lunch the team returned to the airport.

"Marty, Annie and I are going back to Loreto to try to follow up with Padre Papa," Joe said as they arrived at the airport.

"Thanks, you guys. That was a very welcome break," Jack remarked before they departed.

"I hope we can locate Padre Papa without too much trouble. I think he is very active, and I hope we find him at the church," Joe mentioned as they drove back to Loreto.

After a few minutes a voice came over Annie's portable radio calling for a response.

"This is Annie, go ahead caller," she responded.

"Annie, Buck calling," the radio hissed.

"Go ahead Buck, what's up?" Annie responded as Marty and Joe also listened intently.

"You know those black Chevrolet Suburbans you asked

117

us to watch out for? Well, two black Chevy Suburbans just exited the road from San Javier and turned north on Highway 1. They are about ten minutes behind you," Buck reported.

Joe instinctively looked in the rear-view mirror and saw a black shape on the highway headed in their direction. It wasn't more than a minute before two black Suburbans passed the navy van like it was standing still.

"Look up," Marty said after the Suburbans passed.

There were two bright white orbs about 6 feet in diameter rotating counterclockwise and following the Suburbans at approximately one thousand feet altitude. Joe, Marty, and Annie watched as the two Suburbans continued northbound close to 80 miles per hour with two bright rotating orbs following.

"There is no way we can keep up with them. Let's go see if we can find Padre Papa," Joe suggested.

"Annie, would you try to contact Casey and Donna back at Puerto Escondido and let them know about the Suburbans?" Marty asked.

"Sure, Marty, I will try but I'm not sure this portable radio will reach," Annie responded.

"Joe and I will try to locate Padre Papa," Marty said as Joe parked the van in the Santa Casa Church parking lot.

"There's Padre Papa walking across the lot," Joe said as Marty got out and made contact.

"*¿Hola Padre, buenas tardes?*"

"I am good and you?" Padre replied.

"We just wanted to check back with you about activity at Pablo Escobar's compound or any other information you might have about him."

"Yes, I have much to tell you. I was hoping you would return. Let me get your telephone number so I can call you next time, if necessary," Padre Papa responded.

"Sure, Father, here is a number we can be reached at the

Puerto Escondido Navy Base. What have you seen recently?"

"Recently? Well, a few minutes ago I got a report that two large black Chevrolet Suburbans left San Javier and are driving north very fast with the Holy Lights following them."

"We saw that. Where do you think they are going?" Joe asked.

"I am not sure, but I will find out as soon as they stop," Padre Papa answered.

"How do you get this information?" Marty asked.

"From the faithful. The sheep of the flock. They call them 'Holy Lights" and some people call them UFO's or Foo Fighters. Who is to say? If my flock calls them 'Holy Lights' then who am I to say different?" Padre asked. "The people who worship here at The Holy House Church are not sophisticated or educated. Many are underprivileged, uneducated, salt of the earth, children of God. They know that Jesus has a special place in His heart for them and they also know He watches out for them. They follow the Holy Lights because they believe the Holy Spirit of God has a plan and is working to protect them," Padre explained.

"What do you think is going to happen?" Joe asked.

"Only God knows. There is someone else who may help you understand more about the Holy Lights. His name is Abuelo Paco. They say this man is 102 years old. He is a fisherman and has fished the Sea of Cortez since he was a child. He has seen the Holy Lights many times and has stories to tell about them. He can be found at the docks near his *panga* boat "*Pelicano Magico*". He no longer goes to sea, but he supervises his grandsons, who do the fishing. You should talk to him if you have the time. I will call the naval base and report any future information about the black Suburbans to you."

"Oh, I forgot to mention to you that Abuelo Paco only speaks Spanish," Padre added.

"Annie is fluent in Spanish. When she returns, we might

go by the docks and see if Grandfather Paco is there. Thank you for that information, Padre. Here comes Annie now."

"I climbed that hill over there and was able to get through to Casey," Annie reported.

"Padre, before we go would you be kind enough to give us a blessing?" Joe asked.

"Absolutely, Joe, please bow your heads. Lord God in Heaven, your word calls peacemakers the children of God. I ask you to watch over your courageous children. Lead them and guide them to victory over the evils of this world. In Jesus name, we pray," Padre prayed while making the sign of the cross.

"Amen, Padre. Thank you," Joe, Marty and Annie responded.

"Let's go see if we can find Abuelo Paco," Joe said.

"Who?" Annie asked.

"We may need your help speaking to an old fisherman who has stories to tell about the Holy Lights. He only speaks Spanish so bring your Spanish dictionary," Marty said with a smile as they headed toward the docks.

15.

ABUELO PACO

" There at the closest slip to the shore is a white *panga* with the words *Pelicano Magico* written on her bow," Annie declared as she pointed to a heavily built fiberglass *panga* about 25 feet in length, powered by two 50 HP outboard Mercury motors and sporting a Bimini top.

Annie asked two fishermen cleaning the boat and tending the fishing gear if 'Abuelo Paco' was available. She was politely corrected to address him as *Señor* Francisco Perez Castilleja as they walked down the dock to a slightly built, dark complected man with snow white hair protruding from his cone shaped straw hat. Introductions were made in Spanish by Annie, explaining they were visitors to the area and were curious about the Holy Lights. The elderly man with large sad eyes began speaking in halting Spanish with Annie interpreting.

"He apologizes for his Spanish and says he is Monqui Indian and has had very little schooling," Annie interpreted. "He grew up in the Loreto area and has lived all his life here as a fisherman. He says he first saw the Holy Lights in 1960 out on the Sea of Cortez while he was diving for pearl oysters off Cabeza de Mechudo with two other men. It was in the afternoon on Thursday November 10th when the Holy

Lights appeared in the sky at a distance of about 100 meters and an altitude of about 300 meters. He says they were white balls of bright light about 2 meters in diameter and they rotated around each other. He says they watched them for about 30 minutes when all of a sudden a large submarine surfaced under the lights," Annie translated.

"He used some Indian words that I don't understand, but I think I understand the basic idea of what he is saying," Annie reported. "He explains he sometimes receives messages in his head on what other people are feeling or thinking and says he received a clear message from the bright orbs flying above the large submarine. They were concerned about the safety of the whole world," he says.

"About a month later, two U S Navy sailors contacted him and his fellow fishermen regarding the submarine. They had photographs of several submarines and they wanted to know if the submarine they saw was in one of the photographs. They interviewed each one of them separately and they each picked out the same photograph. He heard it was a Soviet November class nuclear powered submarine, according to the photograph," Annie interpreted.

"What happened to the submarine?" Marty asked.

"It was going north, and it went under the water. The Holy Lights also went into the water, following the submarine disappearing down deep into the Canal de San Jose," Annie interpreted.

"The water in the Canal de San Jose is over 3 kilometers deep," he says. "He has also seen strange things in the water in the area southeast of Isla Tortuga or Turtle Island, which is 17 miles east of Santa Rosalia. He has seen the water boil several times in a large area without getting hot. The lights then come up out of the water, go quickly up into the sky and disappear."

"That is about the same location where we saw the orbs enter the water during our flight down to Loreto," Marty remarked.

"What do you think is going on, Annie?" Joe asked.

"All I know is this sweet little man appears to believe everything he's telling us," Annie replied.

"Oh, and he insists I call him 'Abuelo Paco,'" Annie said with a smile. "He says he saw the Holy Lights briefly today as they flew north, following two black Suburbans and he got the impression the orbs were very worried," Annie reported.

"El que la sigue la consigue, He who seeks shall find. *Nadie se va de este mundo vivo*, No one leaves this world alive," Annie interpreted as everyone shook hands with Abuelo Paco and thanked him.

16.

SEAL Team Raids

Back at the Puerto Escondido navy base the team gathered for a meeting. Supervising CIA Case Agent Casey Abbot announced the assaults on Bass Reeves and the San Javier compound would take place soon.

"Bass Reeves was reported to be in relatively shallow waters today about 10 miles west of the Mexican mainland, approaching the village of Topolobampo on the mainland, and is expected to be at about 110 degrees west, 26 degrees north, by this evening. There is a new moon so that should help with the SEAL Teams approaches and the weather is expected to be calm. SEAL team 2 will advance on the San Javier compound while SEAL team 4 will take control of Bass Reeves. We hope to have all 5 nuclear artillery shells in custody before morning," Casey explained.

"I got a call from Padre Papa a few minutes ago with an update on the black Suburbans that left San Javier earlier today. They continue traveling north and are occasionally followed by orbs or Holy Lights, as Padre calls them. His people also continue to follow them, and they will provide us with updates," Annie reported.

"What time will the assaults take place?" Joe asked.

"The SEAL teams will coordinate exactly when they will

make their moves, which should take place within minutes of each other. It could happen any time after dark until morning light," Casey advised.

"What happens following the raids?" Joe asked.

"The teams have been advised to make sure the artillery shells are safe for transport and to bring them here to the Puerto Escondido Mexican Navy Base and turn them over to Captain Hugo Chávez," Casey reported.

"Same thing with the shipment of cocaine," Donna advised.

"I will then contact my superiors to determine what they want to do with the evidence," Hugo advised.

"That seems to be the accepted protocol. Now we wait," Marty advised.

"We should be able to pick up scrambled radio traffic from both SEAL teams on our encrypted portable radios," Donna stated.

"Let's stay close, listening while we wait, in the event a SEAL team needs our help," Joe suggested.

"I have set up two portable radios, each on scramble mode, so we can listen in on the radio traffic of both SEAL teams. Team 2 will be communicating on tactical channel 1, while team 4 will be on tac 2," Casey advised.

"Now we wait," Marty said.

At 9 PM, while everyone was patiently waiting for the portable radios to announce the beginning of the assaults on MV Bass Reeves and the San Javier compound, the squelch on one of the portables broke the silence, "Home base, Home base, Bigfoot calling," a man's voice came from the portable radio on channel 1.

"Go ahead, Bigfoot."

"Home base, can you give us a radio check?"

"You are 5 by 5, Bigfoot."

"10-4, Bigfoot out."

"Home base, home base, Rat Pack calling for a radio check," another man's voice came over channel 2.

"5 by 5, Rat Pack," was the response.

"What's going on Casey? Can you translate that radio traffic for us?" Joe asked.

"Sure, those were radio checks to make sure the radios are in good working order, 5 being the optimum for strength of signal and 5 for clarity of the radio signal. The two teams have chosen the names Rat Pack and Bigfoot. Team Rat Pack will conduct the assault on MV Bass Reeves and Team Bigfoot will assail the San Javier compound at about the same time. Each team will be transported to their respective locations by helo in order to stage, before moving on their targets. At that point they should announce that they have staged. Bigfoot will land 6 SEAL team members to stage a short distance from the San Javier compound. They will then move to take control of the compound. Rat Pack will also travel by helo to a short distance behind MV Bass Reeves where they will stage by deploying their Zodiac inflatable boat. 4 team members will chase down and board MV Bass Reeves. The assaults should take place at about the same time. Since Bass Reeves is further away, Team Rat Pack will have to leave before Bigfoot so that the assaults can be coordinated to happen at the same time," Casey explained.

"When will they start?" Annie asked.

"I'm not sure. We should hear something on the radios when it happens, but it may be a while. My guess is we will hear something before morning," Casey said.

Team members took turns listening to the two radios for activity throughout the night until about 2 AM.

"Rat pack liftoff at 0200 hours," squawked the portable radio.

"Acknowledged Rat Pack, Home base standing by," was the response.

Then an hour later, "Bigfoot liftoff 0300 hours."

"Acknowledged Bigfoot, Home base standing by."

Team members were anxiously waiting for word, drinking

coffee and chatting quietly throughout the night until, "Home base, Home base, Bigfoot staged, helo standing by."

"Acknowledged Bigfoot, 0340 hours."

"Home base, Home base, Rat Pack staged, helo standing by for a return to San Lucas."

"Acknowledged, Rat Pack, 0344 hours."

"Now it begins," Casey stated. "Bigfoot has 6 SEAL team members moving on foot to the San Javier compound and Rat Pack is chasing down Bass Reeves in a Zodiac inflatable to board her and seize control."

"What happens if the SEAL teams run into trouble?" Annie asked.

"The helo's are standing by in the area just in case things don't go well. They will be waiting for word from their teams."

"Home base, Home base, Rat Pack."

"Go ahead, Rat Pack."

"We have secured MV Bass Reeves and have set a course for Puerto Escondido. No casualties."

"Received, Rat Pack. Your helo can return to San Lucas. Home base standing by at 0412 hours."

Then there was silence for what seemed like an hour with everyone glued to the radios wondering what was going on at the San Javier compound until, "Bigfoot helo, Bigfoot helo, Bigfoot calling."

"Bigfoot helo, go ahead Bigfoot."

"Can you land inside the compound in the area east of the single ground flare?"

"On my way, Bigfoot."

"Home base received the Bigfoot radio traffic at 0502 hours."

Then silence again for about 30 minutes.

"Home base, Home base, Bigfoot."

"This is Home base, go-ahead Bigfoot."

"We are aboard the helo and headed to Puerto Escondido. No casualties."

"Home base received at 0533 hours."

"Bigfoot's helo should be arriving in just a few minutes. Let's make sure the landing area is clear and lighted," Casey reported.

The team walked down to the point of land just east of the navy buildings that protruded into the inner bay. The area was as large as a football field and had a nicely maintained lawn outlined in whitewashed grapefruit sized boulders. Two sailors moved several picnic tables and lawn chairs out of the way and turned on some lights that illuminated a large "H" in the center of the field.

All of a sudden a helicopter appeared, flying in low from the north just off the water and between two hills. It quickly flew across a spit of sand known as "the windows," and into Puerto Escondido's inner bay.

It flew directly to the landing zone and landed quickly and effortlessly. It immediately shut down its motor and, while the blade was still turning, 6 men in battle gear exited the helicopter. One soldier approached the team.

"Casey Abbott?" the tall, slim man in his 40's with grease paint all over his face, asked.

"Yes, sir, that's me," Casey replied as he stepped forward.

"Is there somewhere we can debrief?" the soldier asked as the team watched.

"Yes, sir, we can use the Mexican Navy's conference room if you like."

"We have also confiscated some evidence which we need to turn over to you, sir."

"Yes, of course. You can bring the evidence with you to the conference room."

"We could use a transport for the weapons if you have a van or truck. We could back up to unload the helo."

"I can get that for you," Hugo responded as he turned to a sailor and directed him to bring a van to the helo pad.

A navy van was backed up to the helicopter and the soldiers began unloading rifles, wooden boxes of ammunition, metal canisters of more ammunition, hand grenades, rocket propelled grenades, and two large canvas bags. Everyone then walked back to the conference room where the confiscated evidence was displayed on several tables.

"What is your name, sir?" Casey asked the soldier.

"We don't go by names, sir. You can call me Lieutenant. We need to inventory this evidence and then turn it officially over to you. Is that acceptable to you, sir?"

"Yes, of course Lieutenant."

"My men will count and record the serial numbers of all the weapons and provide you with an inventory for you to sign. We will also double count the cash that is in the canvas bags and allow you to do the same before we sign off. Does that sound reasonable, sir?"

"Yes, perfect. Did you see any sign of two nuclear artillery shells?" Casey asked.

"No, sir, we looked specifically for the nuclear shells without success. We checked inside a helo parked inside the compound and then disabled it with some C-4 explosive."

"I notice you have a map and some papers you confiscated from the compound on a table over there. Is that correct?" Joe asked.

"Yes, sir, we had to blow open a walk-in safe where the weapons were stored, and I noticed the map and paperwork on the floor. The shaped explosive charge damaged some of the paperwork and map, but I thought there might be enough left to be helpful to you. Feel free to take a look at it. We should have a completed inventory for you to sign in about an hour. Then it is all yours."

Joe and Marty spread the papers and map out on the table to take a closer look. The map was a worn and stained roadmap of the Baja Peninsula and the northern part of México's border with the United States.

"It appears this map has been folded and unfolded numerous times," Marty observed.

"And whoever looked it over was a coffee drinker. What is

the significance of those 5 dots near the border?" Joe asked.

"They are labeled 1 through 5, and here on this separate piece of paper are what appears to be coordinates for each of the 5 dots on the map," Marty noted.

"Let's check it out. Dot number one has coordinates of latitude 32 degrees, 32 minutes, 9 seconds North; longitude 116 degrees, 34 minutes, 11 seconds West. According to the chart, that puts it just east of the village of Tecate, near the border," Joe said.

"The other locations are near the border too. I wonder what it means?" Marty asked.

"It's hard to tell at this point but it appears there is or will be something important happening at the border. Pablo's black Chevy Suburbans were headed north with the Foo Fighters and Padre Papa's faithful following. I have a very uneasy feeling we may be missing something important. I hope the 5 dots and map coordinates have nothing to do with 5 nuclear artillery shell improvised explosive devices, Marty."

"I agree, but where did the two nuclear shells at the San Javier compound go?"

"Possibly north with the Suburbans. At least the 3 nukes on Bass Reeves have been intercepted," Joe said.

"Yes, Bass Reeves should arrive sometime tomorrow morning," Marty mentioned.

Just then Annie came into the room.

"Hi guys, I just got off the phone with Padre Papa. His people followed the Suburbans north to a location just east of the village of Tecate, near the border. They appear to be getting ready to move again now and Padre Papa said he would keep us posted."

"Does anyone know how to disarm improvised explosive devices like these nuclear shells?" Marty asked.

"I would guess Snake could do it with his Vietnam experience. I will go find him." Joe responded.

The team got together in the cafeteria for the evening

meal with the 6 SEALs and their pilot. Joe, Marty and the team members enjoyed a few minutes of socializing while discussing the past events. The SEAL team members were quiet and polite, addressing each other with only their first names or rank. Several chatted with the Mexican sailors in Spanish, including Lieutenant Veronica who was beside herself in excitement associating with so many "dangerous warriors" at one time. Snake, Veronica, and several Mexican sailors were in a technical conversation in Spanish and English on how to disarm different types of ordinances.

"I don't have any experience disarming soviet made artillery shell IED's. The IEDs I worked on in Vietnam were Chinese," Snake advised before explaining how to defuse a Chinese made IED.

After supper the lists of confiscated evidence from the San Javier compound were explained, reviewed, and accepted. The SEAL Lieutenant signed the inventory "SEAL Team 2 Lieutenant." Casey Abbott signed the inventory documents, accepting custody. Casey then immediately signed over the inventory to Captain Hugo Chávez of the Mexican Navy. There were 15 AK 47 rifles, 4000 rounds of ammunition, 20 RPG's, 20 hand grenades, 5 pounds of C-4 explosives, $300,000. cash in US dollars, 13,000,000. cash in Russian rubles, and miscellaneous papers.

The next morning at 0715 hours the foghorn from MV Bass Reeves sounded 2 short blasts as it approached the Mexican Navy dock at Puerto Escondido.

"*Puerto Escondido Capitán, Puerto Escondido Capitán,* MV Bass Reeves calling on channel 16."

"Go to channel 14, Bass Reeves."

"Bass Reeves howdy on channel 14."

"Welcome to the Puerto Escondido Mexican Navy Station, Bass Reeves, what is your draft please?" Captain Hugo asked.

"The draft on MV Bass Reeves is 27 feet 9 inches or 8.5 meters."

"Received 8.5 meters draft Bass Reeves. You may tie to the navy dock number 2. Sailors are dockside awaiting your arrival."

"Muchas grassy ass, Señor."

17.

MV Bass Reeves

After arriving at the Mexican Navy dock, the 4 SEAL team members marched the ship's captain and 4 crew members at gunpoint off the ship and up to the navy facility. The soldier in charge introduced himself as SEAL Team 4 Lieutenant.

"This is Reginald Lloyd, the captain and owner of the Merchant Vessel Bass Reeves," the Lieutenant stated as he pushed the man forward.

"Hey, take it easy, buster. You don't have to be so pushy," the captain complained.

"What is your name and occupation sir?" Casey asked.

"I am Reginald Higbee Lloyd, captain and owner of this here Merchant Vessel Bass Reeves. I am a British citizen in good standing, and I demand to know why I have been hijacked on the high seas."

"I am Casey Abbott, an agent with the United Stated Federal Government and you are here because we believe you are a threat to the people of the United States and México. Captain Hugo Chávez here is in charge of this Mexican Navy Base. We both want to know what your business is here in Mexican waters, headed north towards the border."

"Well, I picked up a load of fertilizer in Chili consigned

to the Guaymas Farming Cooperative and to be delivered, FOB to Guaymas, Sonora, México. I was headed there when you people boarded my ship, pointed guns at me and my crew like pirates, and forced me to sail here instead of my consigned destination."

"Did you stop anywhere between here and Chili after loading the fertilizer?" Joe asked.

"Who are you?"

"My name is Joseph Creed. I, along with these other people, am a member of a task force of American and Mexican law enforcement personnel with a mission to protect our countries from smuggled drugs and weapons. We are interested in what you are transporting and where your shipments are going."

"My name is Martin Goodson, and I am an FBI agent. I need you to help me understand some things. You appear to be a middle-aged Black man with a British passport and a captain's license and papers that show you are the owner of the Merchant Vessel Bass Reeves. Yet you dress and talk like a cowboy from Western US. You are wearing jeans, cowboy boots, a kerchief, and a cowboy hat. Can you explain these differences to me?" Marty asked.

"Well sure, pardner. I had no idea you all were the law. Shucks, those pirates that took over my ship looked like soldiers, but they showed no markings on their uniforms. I have great respect for law officers, especially western sheriffs, and marshals. Heck, I even named my ship Bass Reeves if that gives you an idea of what I think about law officers."

"I am Annie Diaz, FBI agent. Who is Bass Reeves?"

"You are a law officer, and you don't know who Bass Reeves was? Maybe, young filly, some of these other law officers can fill you in on who the famous Bass Reeves was."

"I know," came a woman's voice from the back of the room.

Everyone turned and looked at Lieutenant Veronica Sabroso, who had a smile on her face.

"Señor Bass Reeves was born into slavery sometime in July, 1838 in the state of Arkansas. He escaped slavery as a young man and went to live with the Indians for several years. After slavery was abolished, Señor Reeves was hired as a Deputy United States Marshal in Indian Territory because he spoke several Indian languages. He was the very first Black US Marshal west of the Mississippi River and in his career, he arrested over 3000 wanted men. He was in many gunfights and killed 14 men during his lifetime. You can have Wyatt Earp, Doc Holliday, Bat Masterson or Pat Garrett. Bass Reeves is my hero!"

"Bravo, young lady! There is much more about this man of the untamed American West you have not mentioned that enlarges his shadow. He needs to be recognized for his integrity and courage," Captain Lloyd explained.

"I agree, but what about your integrity. Why don't you tell us, from start to finish, about your trip from Chili to where you are at now?" Joe asked.

"OK, hoss, I won't fuss about that. I picked up 5000 one hundred-pound sacks of sodium nitrate fertilizer at Arica, Chile consigned to the Guaymas, México Farming Cooperative. My four Mexican crew members and I left Arica, headed for Guaymas with the fertilizer consigned by Señor Pedro Escobar. We sailed without problems to waters off Buenaventura Columbia where I received a radio call from the port captain requesting I hold for 3 hours and expect contact with the consignor, Pedro Escobar, who would arrive shortly by *panga*. Señor Escobar and two other hombres arrived in an hour. They had three boxes of farm implements and two pallets of vegetable seed they wanted to put aboard, bound also for Guaymas, México. I agreed and we got it loaded aboard and headed out again for Guaymas. Pedro Escobar had a Columbian passport and was supposed to be Pablo Escobar's brother, but that was an obvious lie. The other two gentlemen said they held Russian passports and they mostly spoke Russian," Captain Lloyd stated.

"Why do you say Pedro Escobar was lying about being Pablo Escobar's brother?" Joe asked.

"Because he is a gringo and speaks only English. He dresses like an upper-class gringo and his passport was probably counterfeit. There is no way he is Pablo Escobar's brother, and the two Russians were up to no good. One has training in nuclear arms and may be a scientist by the way he talks, and the other is a weatherman."

"How do you know all that?" Joe asked.

"After the war I used to ship freight between Valetta, Malta, in the Mediterranean Sea, to Leningrad, Russia, where I learned to speak some Russian. The two Russians aboard assumed I could not understand them when they spoke among themselves, but I understood enough to figure out a few things about them. The wooden crates of farm implements had the word '*onachoctb*' in Russian stamped on them. Why would they mark those crates with the word danger in Russian, I asked myself? Why would a Russian nuclear scientist and a meteorologist be so interested in getting seed and farm implements to México? If you have any idea who Pablo Escobar is and what he does, why would he associate with a suspicious and slick looking gringo dude with a phony name like Pedro? The answer must be drugs. Pedro was armed with a 9 mm Beretta pistol and even though he did not directly threaten me or my crew it was understood that we needed to do what we were told. When they told me they were expecting two *pangas* to meet up with them just off the town of Topolobampo, Sinaloa, México, I shut down Bass Reeves and drifted offshore and waited for the *pangas*. They off loaded the farm implements and seed to the *pangas* and the last I saw of them, they were headed east, back toward Topolobampo. About two hours later we were boarded by you cops and told to fetch Puerto Escondido. So, here we are. Me and my crew have not broken any laws, we are simple sailors and innocent of any crimes and I demand that you release us immediately and provide me with enough fuel to make Guaymas."

"We are still searching your ship for contraband, so you will have to be patient. How do we know you are telling us the truth?" Marty asked.

"You have the declarations of four crewmembers and me, pardner."

"We need to consider this new information and how it may relate to our mission," Joe declared.

"Captain Lloyd, why don't you and your crew relax for a while, join us for supper and wait until we finish the search of your vessel, so we can decide what to do next?" Hugo asked.

"I guess we don't have too much choice. I do appreciate your hospitality. Please let us continue on our way as soon as possible."

"Let's call the team together to process this new information," Joe suggested.

18.

EVALUATING THE INTELLIGENCE

"So, what information do we have?" Marty asked the team.
"We have 5 nuclear weapons probably headed north towards the US-México border," Casey responded.

"There are 5 coordinates on a map, all near the US-México border," Hugo said.

"We have Foo-Fighters that seem to follow and hover over nuclear armaments and appear to be following Pablo's nukes," Buck advised.

"There are church people following the Foo-Fighters, or what they call Holy Lights, and they report back to Padre Papa in Loreto, and he has agreed to keep us updated," Annie reported.

"The large shipment of cocaine disappeared onto the Mexican mainland at Topolobampo along with the three nuclear weapons," Donna said.

"It stands to reason that there would be a Russian nuclear scientist or technician accompanying the weapons, but what is the reason for a meteorologist? What advantage would Pablo Escobar have by setting off 5 nuclear weapons at the US-Mexican border?" Joe asked.

There was silence.

"I hope you don't mind me listening in," Lieutenant Veronica asked.

"No hay problema, ¿qué estás pensando?" asked Captain Hugo.

"I'm thinking like a drug runner. The first nuke is put near Tecate village, which is east of Tijuana, and the rest are put all across the border almost to the Gulf of México. We know that Pablo Escobar has control of the territory around Tijuana so he can get his drugs to the US, right? If the 5 nukes are exploded along the border when there is a wind out of the northwest, the radiation will make the border area, what do you call it, no man's land? If that happens, besides the death of many innocent people, Pablo Escobar's organization will control the only land border crossing to the US. A very horrible thing for the people at the border, but a very profitable thing for Escobar."

"You may have hit the nail on the head Veronica. A simple exercise in deductive reasoning," Marty exclaimed.

"Probably more like inductive, or bottom up reasoning which only gives us a possibility rather than a probability," Veronica stated.

"One more thing. I want to become part of this team and do what I can to help, if you will have me," she said.

"I guess that would be up to Captain Hugo Chávez, Lieutenant. I would welcome you, but I cannot speak for the others," Joe responded.

"If Captain Chávez agrees to let me join this team, would any of you object?" Veronica asked.

No one objected but several of the team members looked at Snake who was silently staring at the floor.

"I think Lieutenant Veronica Sabroso has come as close as possible to helping us understand Escobar's plans at this point. Let's see if Padre Papa has any more information from his church followers and then we need to determine a plan of action to put a stop to Escobar's evil activities," Joe said as they took a break and disbursed.

"*Adelante,*" Captain Hugo Chávez responded to the

knock on his office door.

"Welcome Señor Snake, what can I do for you?" Hugo said.

"I would like to talk to you about Lieutenant Veronica's request to join the team, if possible, sir," Snake requested, standing in front of Hugo's desk.

"Please, have a seat, Snake."

"I want you to seriously consider not allowing Lieutenant Veronica to join the team. She is too inexperienced and could easily be injured or killed," Snake said as he sat down.

"We all love her, Snake, me like a father and the others like a sister. We would all feel like we would want to die if we lost her. But I cannot say no to her."

"Why not?" Snake asked.

"Because she is a guardian. Her inner, God-given, nature is to protect others, Snake, just like you. It is a gift from God that carries with it the responsibility to exercise that gift. Just as a farmer knows when to harvest, or a fisherman knows where and when to catch fish, a guardian knows when and how to protect. I have already agreed to let her serve on the team, and I put her under the command of FBI Agent Martin Goodson. She objected to being placed under the command of a foreign agent, but I explained to her that I trusted Marty with my life, and she should do the same. Snake, I want a promise you will let her be free to carry out her assigned missions."

"I understand, Captain, I don't like it, but I understand, and you have my assurance regarding Lieutenant Veronica," Snake promised, as he got up to leave Hugo's office with a worried look on his face.

19.

THE PROMETHEUS PLAN

A team meeting was called to plan a course of action based on the information understood at this point. Attending the meeting was: Joe Creed, Marty Goodson, Hugo Chávez, Casey Abbott, Donna Ashford, Snake, Buck Buchanan, Annie Diaz and Lieutenant Veronica Sabroso.

"I think it would be appropriate for Casey to take the lead on this part of our mission, so I will turn the floor over to you, Casey," Joe announced.

"Thank you, Joe, and all of you for being here to help put an end to the threats against the people of México and the United States. I respect all of you for your dedication to your country and for your courage to stand and face the enemy. During this meeting I hope we can put together a plan to stop the threat with the least amount of risk. The least amount of risk first to the people and then to ourselves. I would like us to treat each other in this meeting as equals in rank. Please don't hesitate to suggest any ideas or thoughts you may have," Casey explained.

"Let us outline what we know about the enemy first, then discuss the assets we have and possible methods to achieve the mission to defuse the nukes and stop the threats. What do we know about the enemy thus far?" Casey asked.

"They have five 240-millimeter Russian nuclear artillery shells modified to be IED's. They have a nuclear weapons scientist or technician, a meteorologist and the Escobar cartel's backing," Joe responded.

"They have most probably traveled north already in preparation of placing the nuclear devices at predetermined locations," Annie advised.

"They will probably move away from the area just before the nuclear blasts," Veronica mentioned.

"There are most likely less than 10 men engaged in the placements of the nuclear devices," Marty estimated.

"If Veronica is correct about the nukes causing a deadly radiation in no man's land at the border, then they will probably only explode the nukes when there is a brisk wind out of the northwest, causing a radiation shadow along the border," Snake reasoned.

"Will they set off all the nukes at the same time or will they explode number 1 and then go to number 2 and so forth?" Buck asked.

"I think they may plan to explode first at coordinate number 1 and as the wind carries the radiation southeast, along the border, they may explode number 2 when the radiation cloud arrives and the same with the remaining devices, causing the radiation clouds to combine and increase the destruction," Veronica reasoned.

"Good observations. Now, what assets do we have that can help us in the mission to stop the destruction?" Casey asked.

"Are the SEAL teams still available?" Joe asked.

"Yes, they are ready to go as soon as I issue an order. They also have information about the nukes. We were able to locate schematics and diagrams of the Russian nukes and each SEAL team has one EOD specialist that has practiced several methods of defusing IED's," Casey explained.

"What is EOD and IED?" Veronica asked.

"Sorry, Veronica, I sometimes forget we are communicating in two languages and acronyms are not helpful. EOD stands for explosive ordinance disposal and IED stands for improvised explosive device," Casey explained.

"Where are the Suburbans now?" Marty asked.

"Yesterday Padre Papa told us the black Chevrolet Suburbans were reported to be leaving the Tecate Village area and headed east," Annie responded.

"My guess is they may have placed the first nuke and are moving to place the second one," Marty reasoned.

"Do we have a weather forecast for the Tijuana area for this week and what do we do with Captain Lloyd and the Bass Reeves crew?" Joe asked.

"We have a system moving in tonight with strong winds out of the northeast that will cause problems the entire length of the Sea of Cortez, including Tijuana. We have been trying to get the word out to the fishing fleet. The storm is expected to last several days. I have restricted Captain Lloyd, MV Bass Reeves and crew to the Puerto Escondido Navy base until further notice. I will call the Guaymas Farm Co-op and advise them their fertilizer shipment will be delayed a week," Hugo declared.

"We need to stop the Escobar cartel from placing any more nukes and defuse the ones they have placed as soon as possible," Snake stated.

"If we takedown the group in the Suburbans, we could possibly stop them from sending a signal to explode the nukes. If we corner them, and they had the time, they may set off the nukes before we can gain control," Donna suggested.

"Hit the Suburbans hard and fast is what I'm hearing," Casey said.

"SEAL team Bigfoot should put a stop to the Suburbans while Rat Pack defuses nuke number 1," Joe suggested.

"The storm with high winds may keep the helo's on the ground," Buck mentioned.

"We have two 12 passenger vans here at the naval base. They can transport us north as soon as you like. It appears, however, it will be necessary for us at the naval base to also be prepared for rescue missions from the approaching storm. If you wish, I can arrange for quarters for the teams at Mexican Naval Base number 12 at the Tijuana Airport. I believe I can get us quietly lodged at discreet quarters since I am familiar with the base commander," Hugo advised.

"Why don't you see what you can do Hugo, and let us know. I suggest we head north as soon as we have a base of operations available to us. Does anyone else have suggestions or do we have a plan?" Casey asked.

"This storm worries me; I think Annie and I should stand by the director's aircraft to make sure she stays properly tied down. We can be available after the storm," Buck stated.

It was quiet for a moment until a few team members began nodding and agreeing quietly with Casey's plan to move the operation north to the Mexican Navy Airbase at Tijuana, upon approval.

"You probably already know that the trickster Greek god, Prometheus, stole fire from the king of gods, Zeus. Therefore, I think we should call this the Prometheus Plan, in anticipation of the theft of the nuclear devices," Joe proposed.

The wind was already beginning to pick up.

20.

TIJUANA

A land grant in 1829 initially established Rancho Tia Juana, or Ranch Aunt Jane in English, a large cattle ranch. Tijuana City was later established on July 11, 1889, and it quickly became popular as a tourist destination. The Tijuana airport lies in the Otay borough and is east of Tijuana City center.

"*¿Capitán Hugo, tiene un momento?*" Lieutenant Veronica asked.

"Sure, Lieutenant, how can I help you?"

"I have a dilemma, sir. I want to go north to help the task force stop the attack on our country, but I am not sure I should go."

"Why, Lieutenant?"

"It's because of the storm that is coming. We both know there will be fishermen who will not get word of the storm at their fish-camps, and many will probably need help. I cannot decide if I should stay here and help with rescues or go north with the team."

"You can do both," Captain Hugo suggested.

"Stay here and take command of the rescues, directing activities as needed and when things settle down, turn the mop-up activities over to whomever you think is most capable, then come north and join us. I was about to assign the task to you before you asked. What do you think?" Hugo asked.

"Yes, sir. It is a good plan, and I will do my best. Thank you, sir," Veronica responded.

The Puerto Escondido Navy Base became a beehive of activity as the team packed and prepared to travel north to the navy airbase at the Tijuana airport. CIA Agent Casey Abbott contacted the two SEAL teams, ordering them to ready their helicopters for action and report to the Mexican navy airbase at the Tijuana airport for a team meeting at 1900 hours the next day, if weather permits.

"We better get moving. It will take about 18 hours to get to Tijuana," Snake mentioned to Veronica.

"I'm not going, Snake."

"What, why not? I thought you wanted to join the task force?"

"I do, and I will, but there will be very important work to do here when the storm hits. I will join you as soon as our rescue missions are completed."

"Now I will worry about you even more."

"I will also worry about you, *mi serpiente*. There may be a future for us or there may not; I do not know. You hold a special place in my heart, *mi amor* Snake," Veronica said as they hugged.

The wind out of the northeast continued to increase as the team left Puerto Escondido in two navy vans, traveling north on Baja's Mexican Highway 1. The first van carried the team members while the second van followed, loaded with equipment. They dropped off Buck and Annie at the Loreto airport and then continued north.

"Location number 1, found on the confiscated map from the San Javier compound safe is, 32 degrees, 32 minutes, 9 seconds North; 116 degrees, 34 minutes, 11 seconds West. That is about 3 miles east of the Tijuana airport and it puts us close, but outside the blast zone," Marty stated while looking at the map during the trip.

The team traveled quickly past the villages of Loreto and Mulege, but they stopped for a brief break at Santa Rosalia. Hugo contacted Port Captain Maria Isabel Soto Gonzalez at the Santa Rosalia Marina office.

"*¿Buenas días Isabel, como estas?*" This is Joe Creed from Washington State," Hugo greeted the port captain.

"It is a pleasure to meet you Señor Creed. I am good Hugo. How are things at Puerto Escondido?" Isabel said, politely changing to English.

"Very busy, I was wondering if I could use your telephone, Isabel?" Hugo asked.

"Yes, of course. Would you like a cup of coffee or a cold drink Señor Creed?" Isabel asked as Hugo picked up the telephone.

"I think we only have time for a quick telephone call but thank you Captain, I appreciate the offer," Joe responded with a smile.

"Thank you for the phone calls. We have to run. *Lo siento*, Isabel. I will explain why we are in such a hurry on my way back. Please forgive me," Hugo said as they quickly left the port captain's office.

Back on the road Hugo announced, "Next stop is El Rosario and Mama Espinoza's Restaurant. I made a call to her, and she will have breakfast waiting for us in about 8 hours. I also spoke with Captain Javier Fuerte, at Navy Base 12 – Tijuana, and he is expecting us and has made room for our team. Snake, while we are traveling, would you share with us some information about nuclear arms, what to expect, and safety measures we can take?"

"Yes, sir. I was trained and assigned to an EOD unit in Vietnam and have had some training on nuclear devices and IED's. I can share with you what a nuclear explosion is like, what to expect and some of the defensive tactics you can take to protect yourselves," Snake responded.

"A one kiloton device, like the 240-millimeter Soviet artillery shell, will have a blast kill-zone of about a one-half mile radius at ground level. If it is touched off at altitude it will increase the kill-zone. The shock wave from the fireball travels at about the speed of sound, so if you hear the explosion, the shock wave is immediately on you. If you are at a safe distance, and you see the explosion you will most probably see a double flash. Only nuclear explosions produce the double flash. If you hold your hand up to shield your eyes from the light of the explosion you may be able to see the bones in your hand and the thermal effects will burn your exposed flesh and light your clothing on fire if you are too close to the explosion. The mushroom cloud is also a signature of a nuclear explosion ground burst," Snake explained.

"What about defensive tactics?" Joe asked.

"Bend over and kiss your ass good-by," Snake said with a smile.

"The blast will knock down buildings and toss cars like they are toys. A solid concrete wall, not brick, but solid concrete, may survive the blast, with you behind it. The other consideration is thermal radiation which can not only burn the exposed skin but, due to bleaching pigments in the eye from the flash, blindness can occur for up to 40 minutes. Sunglasses would be helpful in protecting the eyes. Dark clothing absorbs the thermal radiation and may burst into flames whereas light colored clothing can reflect some of the radiation. The explosion will also produce an electronic pulse which will fry electronic circuits, most likely knocking out our radios and radar aboard aircraft nearby, along with the airport radar."

"Thanks, Snake. That should give us some food for thought. Why don't we try to settle down and see if we can get a little rest as we travel across the Sonora desert tonight. We can look forward to a good breakfast at Mama Espinoza's

Restaurant at about daybreak," Casey suggested.

"I should rest like a baby after thinking about what Snake told us," Donna mentioned sarcastically as she adjusted a pillow and tried to find a comfortable position.

21.

La Tormenta

"*La tormenta esta sobre nosotros, teniente,*" a sailor reported as he had difficulty closing the door to the navy base's radio room due to the wind.

"*The storm is not only upon us, it is tearing apart everything that is not tied down,*" Lieutenant Veronica thought to herself.

"*Nortes,*" or winds from the north, are common on the Sea of Cortez. They can blow for several days from the north at 50 miles per hour or better. Waves can be dangerous as the wind from the north has the entire length of the sea to build waves, sometimes more than 20 feet tall.

"*Auxilio, ayúdame, por favor,*" crackled the VHF radio in the Puerto Escondido Navy Base radio room.

That woman's voice sounds familiar, and she sounds desperate, Lieutenant Veronica thought to herself.

After some exchange of information from the woman calling on VHF channel 16 regarding the emergency, Lieutenant Veronica was able to determine that the woman was Leona from the village at Agua Verde and she was terrified for her husband Enrique and others who had been out fishing for 2 days. She had not heard from him, and she was worried that he was caught in the storm. The anemometer mounted on the roof of the navy base radio room was hitting gusts more than 60 miles per hour, Veronica noted.

"Prepare el bote de rescate y pide tres voluntarios," Veronica ordered to make ready the rescue boat and asked for 3 volunteers.

All of Lieutenant Veronica's team wanted to accompany her on the rescue mission so she assigned the task of choosing 3 volunteers to her midshipman. The rescue boat was readied and Lieutenant Veronica, with 3 volunteer sailors, slowly motored through the entrance channel and out onto the raging Sea of Cortez, headed for Enrique's last known location, Isla San Cosme. As soon as the rescue boat left the bay at Puerto Escondido, the wind, spray, and waves immediately threatened to overwhelm and swamp the boat. It was about 18 miles to the small island of San Cosme and the rescue craft was constantly in danger of waves and swells crashing over the stern of the boat, called getting *pooped* in sailor's language. All personnel aboard wore heavy kapok life vests and remained relatively dry and safe inside the cabin as they continued south towards the islands of San Cosme and San Damien.

Puerto Escondido Bay was closed to vessels leaving until further notice. The winds from the northeast increased and the swells, built by the constant wind, also increased to impassable heights. Radio calls from the Puerto Escondido Navy base to Lieutenant Veronica, and rescue boat 121, went unanswered during that time. A telephone call was made to the Tijuana Navy Base on the 2nd day advising Captain Hugo Chávez of the lack of contact with Lieutenant Veronica. Nothing could be done until the storm subsided. The two SWAT teams and their helicopters were grounded at San Lucas waiting to fly north to the navy base at Tijuana to meet up with the team.

"I don't think this windstorm will stop Pablo's men from placing the nuclear artillery shell IED at the first map coordinates. We should reconnoiter that location for any activity as soon as possible," Joe warned.

"I agree. Do we have anyone immediately available with EOD experience?" Casey asked.

"I was cross trained in Vietnam for conventional and nuclear arms," Snake responded.

"How about just Snake and I check out the site before dark?" Casey suggested.

There were no objections or suggestions, so Snake set about locating an unmarked vehicle they could use that would not identify who they were. A well used 1955 Chevrolet pickup with faded paint was borrowed from a sailor to check out the first possible nuclear site.

22.

32° 32' 9" North, 116° 34' 11" West

Tijuana Navy Airbase Captain Javier Fuerte asked, "Casey, do you have a moment?"

"Sure Captain, how can I help you?"

"A sailor asked to be excused for a few moments to provide his pickup truck for you to use. I thought that was strange since you can use any of our navy vehicles here anytime you want."

"Well, Captain, we want to check out a site about 15 kilometers from here near the border that interests us, and we want to appear as discrete as possible."

"Oh, I see. Well, it does not matter what kind of vehicle you drive in the border area. Everyone entering the area is reported to cartel members by the watchers, called falcons, or *halcones*. The cartel gunmen, or *sicarios*, would probably kill you without asking any questions when they saw you were gringos. When I want to go to the border area, I put together two squads of highly trained and well-armed navy sailors. Is there something I can help you with?" Captain Fuerte asked.

"Maybe. We need to take a close look at the area of and

around these coordinates," Casey said as he wrote down the map coordinates.

"Let's take a look at this location on the map in my office."

"OK, I will go get Snake and meet you there."

A few minutes later, in Captain Fuerte's office, the men gathered around a large table of charts.

"This penciled X is: 32° 32' 9" North and 116° 34' 11" West on this chart," Captain Fuerte stated.

"It appears to be a small hill according to the contour lines," Snake said.

"I think I know that location. If I am correct there is a small shack at the top of that knoll used by spotters watching border patrol activities on the US side," Captain Fuerte said.

"What is it that interests the CIA in a border spotting shack?" Captain Fuerte asked.

"I can't go into much detail captain, but that shack may be set up with booby traps to take out anyone that gets close and there may be an IED inside the shack the agency needs to acquire. How can I safely get to that location?"

"I can put together two teams of sailors to make an incursion to the area by force, if necessary, or I can contact the local cartel teniente or lieutenant and ask permission."

"How about a face-to-face meeting with the local cartel lieutenant?"

"Give me a few minutes to make some phone calls," Captain Fuerte responded as he picked up his telephone.

"OK, you have an appointment with a local cartel teniente. We are to show up at Chico's Cantina in Pueblo Maritza, east of here at 1600 hours," Captain Fuerte said after he hung up the telephone.

"I will be accompanying you with a couple of armed sailors as security. When you go into the cantina you will be on your own, with security just outside," Captain Fuerte warned.

A driver and two navy sailors, armed with rifles, arrived

at Captain Fuerte's office with the keys to a navy van a few minutes later. Captain Fuerte, Casey, Joe and Snake got into the van and headed for Pueblo Maritza and Chico's Cantina to meet with a cartel leader.

"There it is, Chico's Cantina. My kind of place," Snake joked as they approached the village.

"How good is your Spanish?" Captain Fuerte asked as the Mexican navy vehicle parked near the cantina.

"Not that good. Would you help us speak to this cartel lieutenant in Spanish?" Casey asked.

"Sure, I'll be happy to help," Captain Fuerte responded as they approached the entrance to Chico's Cantina.

"This place reminds me of Stockman's Bar in Yakima, or maybe a combination of Stockman's and the Alaska Corral Topless Bar," Snake mused as they looked the place over upon entering.

A juke box playing dance music while a thin woman in her 30's, wearing a bikini, pole danced to the beat of the music. Two elderly men sat at the bar drinking beer with several empty bottles in front of them, oblivious to the dancer, talking to each other. The place smelled of beer and urine combined with recently fried food.

Joe, Snake, Casey and Captain Fuerte took a seat at a large table near the entrance. The bartender, a man about 50 years old, wearing dirty jeans, cowboy boots, a stained white T-shirt and an old faded green apron approached the table.

"*¿Qué quieres?*" he asked, staring at the men.

Captain Fuerte ordered 4 bottles of Tecate beer in Spanish.

"We have to open our own beer?" Casey remarked.

"I ordered it that way for your protection," Captain Fuerte advised.

"You don't want to give the bartender the opportunity to slip you a mickey," Snake agreed, grinning.

A door behind the bar opened and three men walked out

around the bar and approached the table where Joe, Snake, Casey, and Captain Fuerte sat.

"*¿Como esta Capitán?*" the largest of the 3 men asked. He was wearing sunglasses, tan Halston designer polyester slacks, a colorful silk Hawaiian shirt, and brown two-tone saddle shoes. His long dark hair with bushy sideburns was tied in a ponytail. The other two men were in their 20's and they were wearing blue jeans and short sleeve unbuttoned shirts, exposing bare chests and gold chains. They had large bulges under their shirts and said nothing but paid close attention to the flashily dressed man in sunglasses.

"*¿Bien y ustedes? Siéntate,*" Captain Fuerte responded as the 3 Mexican men took seats at the table.

"Who is in charge?" Casey asked while looking at Captain Fuerte.

"I am *Teniente* Pulpo, and these are my men, Carlos and Manuel."

"You speak good English," Casey responded.

"Yes, who are you?"

"My name is Casey, and I would like to speak confidentially with only you," Casey stated.

"Let's us go to that table over there," Pulpo suggested.

Pulpo and Casey spent the next 10 minutes quietly talking to each other.

"So, tell me Señor Casey, who the hell are you anyway? You got enough juice to get the Mexican Navy off their butts which means you got some pull from somewhere. Talk to me, *hombre*, and tell me who you *really* are," Pulpo stated quietly.

"I'm with the agency and we are not fooling around. I've got something to tell you and you can believe me or not. It's up to you," Casey frowned while looking Pulpo directly in the eye.

"Yea, shit. You got something important to tell me Mr. CIA and it's for my own good, right? I am supposed to believe everything you tell me, *correcto,* agency man?"

"You can believe what you like. I would hope you and your men would help us, but you can do what you want. What I have to tell you will not be a secret in the near future. If you don't believe me now, I guarantee, you will soon."

"OK, Mr. Spook. Tell me your bullshit, and I will let you know what I think. I have to warn you, however, I grew up in East LA and I cannot recall a cop *ever* telling me something that was true."

"I am not a cop. I am an agent with the United States Central Intelligence Agency, I will publicly deny that, of course, even though it is true. What I have to say is honest, and it will have a negative effect on your life and your current business. I assume you know the name Pablo Escobar?"

"Yes, I know that bastard. Six months ago, his people killed three of my men. He has not caused us any problems in the last few months, but he is an enemy."

"I suspect you also know he wants to control your territory here at the border and, even though he has not disturbed you recently, do not think he has given up on the idea. He has a plan that will not only wipe out you and your cartel, but he will have complete control of the border from the Pacific Coast to the Gulf of México."

"We control the entire border, except for the Tijuana area. Pablo has pushed his way in at Tijuana and taken out several of our men in doing so, but he does not have enough strength to continually control the entire border like we do."

"He will when his plan is enacted. You will no longer be a worry to him Pulpo. He will have a complete monopoly control of both sides of the entire border area. You see, he has plans to make this area from east of the village of Tecate to the Gulf of México a no-mans-land, affected by deadly radiation. Anyone who enters the no-mans-land will sicken and die from radiation poisoning. According to our intelligence, the spotters shack on the little knoll we are interested in is where the first of five nuclear explosions will occur."

"Where does Pablo get five nuclear bombs? You can't just buy those bombs and who would sell them anyway?"

"Our best information is that Pablo bought five nuclear artillery shells from a rogue Russian military scientist, and they have armed them by improvising the shells to explode either with a timer or some remote method. We think he plans to have the nuclear shells placed along the US-Mexican border, from east of Tecate village all the way to the Gulf of México. The map coordinates we intercepted tell us exactly where he plans on having the nuclear IED's placed. We want to see if the first device has already been placed in the spotters shack."

"We can go now and look," Pulpo said loudly as he stood up.

"There's one other thing. It has been reported there may be Foo Fighters following the nukes," Casey mentioned.

"That's a joke, right? What's a Foo Fighter?" Pulpo asked as he sat back down.

Casey spent a few more minutes explaining some, but not all, of the details of the mission. Pulpo then began speaking to his men rapidly in Spanish and the men stood up while Captain Fuerte explained in English,

"It looks like we are all going now to visit the coordinate location with *Teniente* Pulpo leading the way.

"Here, fly these white flags on your vehicles as you follow me to the spotters shack to keep from being stopped by my *companeros*," Pulpo said as he handed the flags to the sailors.

It took about 20 minutes to arrive at the spotter's shack. The vehicles all parked at the base of the small hill, after traveling a couple of miles on a dirt road. The men gathered together to determine what to do next.

"I'm going to hike up there and take a look," Snake said.

"I'll go with you," Casey responded.

"So will I," Pulpo and Joe said in unison as they began walking up the hill.

"Keep your eyes peeled for wires or other signs of snares or traps," Snake warned as they walked up the hill.

The shack was made of plywood, pieces of scrap wood, and tarpaper. It sat at the top of a dusty knoll that rose above the desert floor about 100 feet. The small hill was rounded and close to 2 acres in size with some Octillo plants, Cardon cacti, and one large Boojum tree. The shack was constructed with long, narrow openings on the north side which allowed cartel spotters, or *halcones*, to observe and report by radio to the coyotes, or smugglers, the location of US Border Patrol Officers and activity along the 3 miles of border visible from the shack. The shack had an old battered door on the south side which allowed the falcons to discretely come and go without being seen from the north.

Pulpo pulled a .45 Colt semi-auto pistol from under his shirt and the two *sicarios* followed the group carrying rifles. The windstorm was blowing dust around covering any recent footprints in the area of the shack. Everything around the area looked lifeless. Snake, Casey and Joe looked into the shack through some cracks in the boards and it appeared empty. They carefully entered through the door, looked around and found nothing of interest.

"I don't think they've been here yet," Snake reported.

"I think you are right," Joe responded.

"I can post falcons out there in the desert and contact you if anyone comes around," Pulpo proposed.

"That would be very helpful. There isn't much we can do now except wait," Casey advised as he handed a piece of paper with a telephone number to Pulpo.

"I'll kill those bastards if I see them around here," Pulpo threatened as he handed to Casey a card with some numbers and Spanish words written on it.

"Give that to Captain Javier Fuerte," Pulpo requested.

"We want them to think they have placed the explosive without incident so that we can disarm it, arrest them, and take them into custody. We want to capture the Russian and anyone assisting the deployment of the devices so we can interrogate them. Please, Pulpo, don't take any actions, just give me a phone call if your falcons see activity around the shack." Casey asked.

"OK, Mr. Spook man. I will personally call you and let you hit them first, but after that, those *hombres* are mine."

Back at the Tijuana Mexican Navy airbase Marty was on the telephone to Padre Papa at the Santa Casa Church in Loreto, Baja.

23.

THE SPOTTERS SHACK

"¿Hola Padre, como esta?"

"I am good, Señor Marty. I am happy to talk to you because I have some important information about the Holy Lights."

"What can you tell me, Padre?"

"The faithful people of our church followed the Holy Lights for several days as they traveled north on highway 1 to Tijuana. That is where they are now staying since the big storm arrived."

"Are they all still in Tijuana at this time?"

"Yes, they will call me if the black station wagons leave. They call me at the end of each day to report what has happened and to pray. I will call you, Señor Marty, as soon as I hear from them again."

"Good, thank you, Padre. We hope to put a stop to their activities soon and I really appreciate your help."

"Da nada, Señor Marty. I pray for your success and your safety, *adiós."*

"Goodbye, Padre, I look forward to hearing from you again."

Joe, Snake, Casey and Captain Fuerte returned to the Tijuana Mexican Naval Airbase and provided an update to the rest of the team as to their recent activities with cartel Lieutenant Pulpo and that they could expect a call if any activity is observed at the spotters shack. Just then the telephone rang. Captain Fuerte answered and began a conversation in Spanish.

After a few minutes of conversation, Captain Fuerte hung up and stated, "I have some good news for Captain Hugo and the team regarding Lieutenant Veronica. She was on a rescue mission for fishermen stranded by the storm on Isla San Cosme and her base lost contact with her for two days. She found the stranded fishermen on the lee side of the island where they had beached their *pangas*. All were well, but the *pangas* had been drenched, which drowned their outboard motors and shorted out their radios. She is taking the fishermen to Agua Verde where they will get the necessary tools and supplies to return to their beached boats to retrieve them, now that the storm is easing. She is on her way to Puerto Escondido and asked her base to telephone San Lucas and ask them to hold the helos for her so she can travel with them here to the Tijuana Mexican Naval Airbase. We can expect the two helos with Lieutenant Veronica and the SEAL teams to arrive here in a day or two."

"We need to put together a plan and a contingency to stop the deployment of the nuclear IED at the spotters shack. If we need to move on the spotters shack before our SEAL teams arrive, we should have a plan to use Captain Fuerte's men, then another plan if the SEAL teams are available to us," Joe advised.

"My guess is that we will see two black Chevrolet Suburbans approach the shack after dark and attempt to deploy the IED soon," Joe continued.

"I can have 4 fully armed assault teams ready to go at a moment's notice. I will alert my men now to be ready to move when needed," Captain Fuerte responded.

"Good, our goal is to contain the Suburbans and truck

and not allow them to leave. We then need to locate and defuse all five IED's immediately, if necessary. If there is a problem and we are not able to locate or defuse the nukes immediately then governments on both sides of the border must be alerted for an evacuation of civilians," Casey advised.

"Two SEAL team members are experienced with EOD, but what if we have to move on the spotters shack before the helos and SEALs arrive?" Casey asked.

"This facility has no one with the skills to defuse the IEDs," Captain Fuerte responded.

"I think I can do it. I am EOD trained from Vietnam where I helped with explosive ordinance disposal on several occasions. I received some nuke training at the same time," Snake reported.

"I hope we have time for our SEAL teams to arrive and prepare for the assault on the spotters shack, but we do have Snake, if necessary," Joe stated.

The tension and apprehension of a possible nuclear explosion nearby, although unspoken, was on everyone's mind. Bunkers and safe locations from a nuclear blast were noted. Local and federal government agency information and telephone numbers for both sides of the border were posted in the event an evacuation order was necessary. They then waited for the helo's with two US Navy SEAL teams and Lieutenant Veronica to arrive from San Lucas. They also waited for word from cartel Lieutenant Pulpo that the black Chevrolet Suburbans had arrived at the spotters shack.

The telephone in Captain Fuerte's office rang.

"*Bueno, momento*. It is for you," Captain Fuerte said, handing the telephone to Marty.

"Si, yes, Father. OK, gracias Padre. Yes, thank you," Marty replied to the caller after listening for a few moments.

"That was interesting. Padre Papa says he has received calls from people in the area of the City of Hermosillo in the State of Sonora, that the Holy Lights have been spotted nearby on several occasions. They appear to be following two vehicles, a yellow farm truck and a white Chevrolet Suburban with dark windows. The truck and the Suburban were last seen going northbound on highway 15. Padre Papa has alerted people in the northern towns to watch for the Holy Lights and to immediately notify him if they are seen."

"That could be the three nukes and shipment of cocaine that left MV Bass Reeves off the coast of Topolobampo. According to Captain Lloyd, there were two Russians, a gringo named Pedro Escobar, who is the presumed brother of Pablo Escobar, and two *sicarios* on loan from Pablo Escobar on board. If they all left Bass Reeves with the nukes and cocaine. It would only seem reasonable that they would connect with the two Suburbans that left Pablo's San Javier compound a few days ago," Joe surmised.

"If they leave Highway 15 and take Highway 2, then we know they are coming this way and it will take them a few hours," Hugo said.

"Meanwhile, let's hope the helo's with the 2 SEAL teams arrive soon," Snake stated.

"I will stay close to this telephone and let you know if anything develops. Meanwhile, why don't you collect your thoughts and try to get some rest. Things could get difficult soon and your minds to be sharp," Captain Hugo suggested as the team disbursed.

Joe found a payphone near the base market.

"Yes operator, please reverse the charges. Hello, Lydia, can you hear me?" Joe spoke loudly into the telephone.

"I know I told you I would be home by now, but some other things have occurred and I need to stay for another week or two."

"I don't understand, Joe, you're an insurance investigator, not a law enforcement officer. Why do you have to remain there when your original mission with Marty has been completed?" Lydia asked.

"I need to give Marty a hand if he needs it and I am involved with insurance work, actually. It's called mitigation of possible future claims," Joe explained.

"OK, please come home soon, Joe. I love you and I miss you."

"I will, Lydia. I promise. I love you too."

The team members gathered in the cafeteria for a cup of coffee and a snack and began discussing the possible future events.

"Has anyone witnessed an actual nuclear explosion?" Hugo asked.

There was silence except for the sound of plates and silverware clinking from the kitchen, when Snake spoke up and said, "I haven't seen a nuke blast, but I received a fair amount of training when I was in Vietnam, and I can add to what I previously explained. Frrom what I understand, the Russian 240-millimeter artillery shells are at the 1 kiloton range. That means there will be complete destruction of everything within a half mile of the hypocenter of the blast. Heat and the force of the blast will cause everything nearby to vaporize to its molecular form. The shock wave starts within the blast and moves out at just under the speed of sound, causing a distortion of the light from the blast, making it look like a double flash. The double flash is a signature of, and unique to, a nuclear explosion. Besides light rays coming from the blast there are thermal or heat rays, X-rays, and other radiation. Like I explained earlier, if you hold your hand in front of your eyes during a nuclear explosion the X-rays will allow you to see all the bones in your hand and the heat radiation will burn the skin in varying degrees, depending on your distance from the hypocenter. If you look directly at the light from the blast you can be blinded. The rods and cones at the back of the eye can be bleached due to the extreme brightness of the flash, causing temporary blindness. The fireball and mushroom cloud are also a signatures of a nuclear ground burst. The shock wave can be extremely destructive the closer to the blast one might be, and the pressures from the shockwave are much higher than a conventional explosion. The overpressures and blast winds cause most of the damage to structures and to humans. The pressure waves move through a human body causing damage where there is a difference in the densities, like between bone and tissue or between the ribs and the airspace in the lungs. The pressure wave causes air-embolisms and hemorrhaging that quickly become fatal."

"We are far enough away from the spotters shack that we should only receive minimal damage if it actually happens. The concrete structures here should withstand the blast but we must remember the other effects of a nuclear blast and to protect ourselves," Hugo explained.

"This area on both sides of the border is minimally populated so if there is a possibility of an explosion the people could be evacuated without too much disorder. We have the contact information for the border county offices and other government agencies ready for notification, if necessary," Marty noted.

"I hope we are able to contain the 3 Suburbans, the yellow stock truck, and make sure all the artillery shells are defused, without turning it into a running gun battle, or worse," Casey remarked.

"Right now, it feels like the calm before the storm," Joe predicted.

24.

TERROR AT THE BORDER

Snake walked up to Joe and whispered quietly in Joe's ear, "May I talk to you in private for a couple of minutes?"

"Sure, Snake. Let's step outside. What's up my friend?"

"I've got to tell you about something. You remember when Sniffer and I were in the old Chinese tunnels under the City of Yakima with Father Pat?"

"How could I forget. You guys were a mess and your hair turned white in a month. You never did say much about what happened in those tunnels."

"We didn't say much because Father Pat swore us to secrecy. I've kept what happened to myself for a long time and it has bothered me. This mission was foretold to us in the tunnel."

"What did you see?"

"You remember when we began to enter, and a foul smell came out of the tunnel? Then, when we were a ways down the tunnel to the north, a growling noise was heard but we couldn't tell where it was coming from?"

"I remember that, and then the three of you disappeared for about an hour. We couldn't raise you on the radio. Where were you?"

"We were in some sort of paralyzed condition, and it seemed as if time went quickly. We watched something that looked like a large movie screen in color that filled the entire tunnel ahead of us. What we saw was horrifying. People were being burned alive from a bright double flash of light, a huge fireball and mushroom cloud that was overflowing with fire. It made me sick to watch."

"You looked sick when you came out of the tunnel. Where did the black ash that covered all of you come from?"

"When the screen shut down it did so in a whoosh of air that swept past us. The air was freezing cold, and the ash settled out of the air and landed on us. My spirit seemed drained from the event. Father Pat asked us to kneel while he said some prayers and then he asked us to promise him we would keep the events to ourselves. The gloomy, damp feeling in the tunnel began to brighten and warm up as we walked back to the entrance. We then took baths or showered with holy water added to remove the ash residue. It would not come off unless we used holy water. I have not told a soul about that mission until I spoke with Padre Papa not too long ago in Loreto about my promise. Since Father Pat has passed on, Padre Papa said my promise to him is no longer required."

"That is astonishing, Snake. Do you really think what you saw was predicting the future?"

"Yes, everything is falling into place."

"What do you think will happen to you and the rest of us? Did the prediction give you a clue?"

"I think it predicted my death by a nuclear blast. But I reject that outcome, Joe. I will do everything in my power to do my duty and to survive. I just wanted to share that experience with someone I trust. Who knows what the future holds, Joe?"

"God only knows my good friend, and He knows you and the good things you have done in your life," Joe declared as they walked back into the cafeteria.

While Captain Javier Fuerte was checking the weather

forecast, the second line on his office phone lit up. The caller asked to speak with Martin Goodson.

"*Bueno, Señor Marty?* This is Padre Papa."

"Yes, Father, how can I help you?" Marty responded.

"I have information on the Holy Lights. They are approaching your area, traveling northwest on Highway 2. The yellow stock truck and white station wagon are traveling together. The Holy Lights are following them from a high altitude. They may arrive soon," Padre Papa explained.

"Thank you, Padre. Please keep us updated if you hear anything more."

"I will. Bless you and your team, we are praying for your success," Padre Papa said before he hung up.

"What is the weather forecast for the rest of today and tomorrow?" Marty asked Captain Fuerte.

"I just checked, and we are still getting gusts up to 102 kilometers per hour. According to the forecast, the windstorm is expected to last another day and then the wind will diminish over 3 more days."

"Let's get everybody together now. Things may be happening soon," Marty stated.

Team members responded to Captain Fuerte's call to meet immediately in the cafeteria.

"May I have your attention please? Are interpreters available for Spanish-English and vice versa?" Casey asked as he stood up and faced the team. "Things are starting to happen. Padre Papa predicts the white Suburban and yellow stock truck, northbound on Mexican highway 2, may be arriving soon. If we get an alert from Pulpo that the cartel falcons are observing activity at the spotters shack, we will need to move quickly. We expect they will be meeting up with the two black Suburbans from Pablo Escobar's San Javier compound. The last we heard, the black Suburbans were waiting in Tijuana. We have made a number of assumptions about this group's activities, and we could be wrong about the details, so we will need to be on our toes and prepared to make changes to our plan as things progress. The weather is not cooperating. We expect this windstorm to continue for at least another 2 days which precludes the arrival of the two SEAL teams from San Lucas. We assume they will continue to wait out this storm and arrive here when the winds permit. That leaves us without an explosive ordinance disposal technician and two experienced combat SEAL teams to deal with the cartel gunmen. We may need to confront this threat on our own, without much help. I intend to postpone notifying the US and Mexican governments of the nuclear threat until we actually have eyes on the nukes. Our goal will be to stop the deployment, confiscate and neutralize the five nuclear artillery shells by force, if necessary, and take the perpetrators into custody for the Mexican justice system to deal with. We are also interested in a reported shipment of cocaine that may be transported in the white Suburban or the yellow stock truck. Let's first do a review of our assets and then assemble a plan," Casey concluded.

"I can deal with the disposal of armed nukes. I have reviewed the diagrams and schematics translated from Russian and I have some experience in defusing IED's," Snake advised.

"Good Snake. You will be our EOD person. Will you need an assistant?" Casey asked.

"No sir, it is pretty much a one-person job."

"We have two teams of six Mexican Navy sailors. Each team is deployed in 4-wheel drive pickup trucks with two more teams available, if needed. The sailors are armed with M 14 rifles, RPG's and hand grenades," Javier stated.

"We also have, Hugo, Snake, Casey, Donna and me," Joe added.

"You may not know, gentlemen, that I am a former US Army Ranger trained in the operation of a plethora of weapons, close combat, direct fire battles and have had more experiences from Vietnam than I care to think about. Please feel free to assign me to the mission tasks that can best use my skills," Donna Ashford reported.

"That is the reason I asked Donna to be assigned to this mission. She is not very talkative or outgoing, but you can count on her if things go bad," Casey said with a smile.

"The telephones are not working. We cannot call out or receive calls," Hugo announced.

"Presumably caused by the windstorm. How will Pulpo let us know if the Suburbans show up at the spotters shack with the telephones out of service? Joe asked.

"Pulpo gave me the portable radio frequency the falcons use to contact him from their lookout locations since phone service is not the best. I can ask our communications sergeant to monitor the frequency and keep us updated," Captain Javier Fuerte said.

"We will not be able to get updates from Padre Papa as to the location of the yellow stock truck and the white Suburban if the telephones are not working," Marty advised.

"There is a chance the Foo Fighters or Holy Lights will alert us. I'm not sure how dependable the Foo Fighters might be, but we should keep a lookout for them," Joe suggested.

"I agree, Joe. Let's discuss how we should respond if the Suburbans show up at the spotters shack during this windstorm, without us having the assistance of the SEAL teams," Marty advised.

"Our main goal should be to neutralize and seize the nuclear weapons as soon as possible," Casey stated.

"I suggest once we know for sure there are nuclear IED's at the spotters shack, the US and Mexican government agencies within a 10-mile radius should be immediately notified to initiate civilian evacuation procedures," Joe remarked.

"I have the telephone numbers of the US and Mexican government agencies to contact regarding a civilian evacuation, but with the telephones lines down, I am not sure how we can alert everyone," Captain Fuerte reported.

"We may not be able to issue a warning, Captain Fuerte. The only thing I can think of would be to notify the radio and television media in the area," Joe proposed.

"I can prepare to send Mexican Navy sailors to the various media outlets with a message of a possible nuclear incident at the border with a 10-mile destruction and radiation zone," Captain Fuerte responded.

"That may be the best we can do. What about the evacuation area above the border in the US; how could they be notified?"

"I will work on that. Any suggestions will be appreciated." Captain Fuerte said.

"How about sending a Mexican Navy messenger to contact the US Border Patrol at the Tijuana crossing?" Donna suggested.

"Good idea, Donna. We need to plan on how we should respond if the Suburbans show up at the spotters shack before the SEALs are able to travel from San Lucas to Tijuana. If there are two black Suburbans traveling east from Tijuana and a yellow truck and a white Suburban traveling west to meet at the spotters shack, we need to also approach from both directions to keep them from turning back or escaping. Once we are able to control the area our first priority would be to determine the status of the nukes. We need to know if any are armed and, if so, they need to be neutralized. Any wounded will need to be tended to and Captain Fuerte needs to be notified if we believe a civilian evacuation is required," Casey said.

"Do we have enough portable radios for everyone?" Joe asked.

Portable radios were passed out among the participants with the suggestion they be fully charged and tuned to the same frequency that was provided. A map of the area was used to determine the routes the different team members would take when approaching the spotters shack should it be ordered that the assault would take place without the help of the two US Navy SEAL Teams. Ten young Mexican Navy sailors in fatigues had been listening to the interpreter explain what was being said.

"Keep your radios turned off until we need them because a nuclear blast will disable them if they are on," Snake advised.

"What do we do if the SEAL teams arrive in time for the assault?" Donna asked.

"We let them make and execute their own plan with us assisting," Casey responded.

"If everyone is packed up and ready, all we have to do now is wait," Joe stated.

"*La radio está hablando,*" a sailor entering the room reported to Captain Fuerte.

"There seems to be some radio traffic on the Falcon's frequency that we are monitoring. Let's go listen in," Captain Fuerte suggested.

Hugo, Casey, Joe, Snake, Donna and Captain Fuerte gathered around the shortwave radio in the base radio room. It was quiet for several moments until a man's voice erupted speaking Spanish rapidly, ending in a laugh. Another man's voice responded with another laugh. Then silence.

"Sounds like they are getting bored," Hugo mentioned as he took a seat in the corner of the room.

"Are the telephones still down?" Joe asked.

"Yes, we check them every few minutes. They are still down. I have also stationed a sentry to observe the skies for any lights or abnormal activity and I have prepared written messages to the various government agencies and media outlets, bearing my notarized signature, concerning the nuclear threat and suggestion for evacuations and will send them out with sailors if the need arises," Captain Fuerte advised.

The team members chatted quietly among themselves for some time while listening for radio transmissions from the cartel falcons until someone was heard descending the stairs from the roof of the radio room. A young Mexican Navy sailor stood in the doorway with an expression of terror on his face.

"*Capitán Fuerte, ¡hay luces extrañas en el cielo hacia el este!*," announced the sailor excitedly.

"It appears he sees some strange lights in the sky to the east," Captain Fuerte reported.

About that time the radio traffic in Spanish picked up between the two falcons and they did not sound like they were joking or laughing.

"The falcons also see the lights moving towards them from the east," Hugo reported.

"It looks like it is about time to go to work," Donna said, as some of the team listened to the falcons, while others went to the roof of the radio room to see the lights for themselves.

"Yes, it will take us a while to get to the spotters shack so we should head that way now," Joe responded.

"Hugo and I will each take charge of a 4-wheel drive pickup of armed sailors. I will head east and attempt to come in behind the white Suburban and yellow truck while Hugo's men follow up behind the two black Suburbans from Tijuana." Captain Fuerte stated.

"If this turns into a firefight, please remember your crossfires and the location of friendlies so we don't shoot each other," Joe reminded them as they were leaving the radio room.

Joe, Snake, Donna and Casey went to the 12-passenger navy van that transported them, their weapons, and equipment to Tijuana. The radio room operator was asked to keep the team updated with information from the falcons and location of the lights via their portable radios.

"We will go east on Mexican highway 20 and then circle around and come back west on highway 2 behind the white Suburban and yellow stock truck, if possible," Captain Fuerte advised.

"We will wait for the two black Suburbans to pass us going east on highway 2 and then we will discreetly follow them. The only escape routes they may have are to go north or south. If they run north, they will come to the US-Mexican border, and if they go south, they will be in the desert," Hugo responded.

"We will be in the 12-passenger van following Hugo. We all need to keep updated and in contact with each other on our portable radios," Casey said as they walked to the vehicles.

"Navy radio reports the lights are about 5 miles east of the spotters shack at this time and moving slowly west," Captain Fuerte announced over the portable radios.

"There goes the two black Suburbans. They just passed by us, eastbound on highway 20. We are following at a distance," Hugo reported over the radio.

"Give them plenty of room so we don't alert them. We believe we know where they are going," Casey announced.

The next 30 minutes went by slowly with no radio traffic or announcements as the teams continued to move toward their respective positions. An excited and rapid announcement came over the portable radios in Spanish.

"Navy radio states the falcons have observed a yellow truck approaching the base of the hill where the spotters shack sits," Captain Fuerte reported over the radio.

"The two black Suburbans are still about 10 minutes away, with us following about a mile behind them. Let's give them about 5 minutes after they meet before we make our entrance," Casey reported.

"Acknowledged," responded Hugo and Captain Fuerte.

The exact location of the spotters shack, the Suburbans, and yellow truck were easily visible to the approaching team members because the Foo Fighters or Holy Lights were shining brightly in the night sky, rotating counter-clockwise at about 3000 feet altitude.

"¿*Ves eso?*" (Do you see that?) came over the team's portable radio.

"Foo Fighters. They are on our side," reported Snake over the radio followed by a translation in Spanish by Hugo.

Approaching closer, the team could see people at the top of the knoll near the spotters shack. Hugo's pickup stopped at about 100 yards distance from the base of the knoll, as did Casey driving the 12-passenger van behind him.

Round muzzle flashes of light were seen coming from the figures near the spotters shack and at the same moment the van got hit several times with gunfire.

"Take cover, they are shooting at us!" came the report over the team radio.

The sailors in the back of Hugo's pickup scrambled out and took cover behind the wheels and motor block as bullets continued hitting the vehicles. Casey, Joe and Snake crawled out the passenger door and also took cover. At that moment two loud gunshots were heard nearby.

"Where's Donna?" Snake asked.

They all looked to see Donna standing about 20 feet away from the driver's side of the van in a shooting stance, 90 degrees to the knoll, with her cheek firmly placed against the stock of the M-14 rifle. She was taking her time aiming at the shooters.

"*Bang*"

Then after a moment,

"*Bang*"

Donna then walked around to the passenger side where the men were taking cover and said, "I got two of them up on the knoll but there are at least four more down by the yellow truck. Why don't we lob an RPG over to the far side of that truck where they are hiding?"

"Hugo, can one of your men put a rifle propelled grenade

in behind that yellow truck where they have taken cover?" Casey asked over the radio as more rounds hit the van and Hugo's pickup.

"We have an easy shot with an RPG from where we are," Captain Fuerte reported.

"Go for it, sir!" Casey responded to Captain Fuerte over the radio.

Joe looked into the night sky above the knoll and noticed that the Foo Fighters had disappeared. At the same moment a *"Pop"* was heard coming from the east while a trail of sparks shot into the sky and arched downward, landing just behind the yellow stock truck with a loud *"Boom"* and flash that lit up the night sky. Then there was silence.

"¡Dejen sus armas!" was announced, ordering the men to put down their weapons.

Two men began yelling in Spanish from behind a black Suburban, near the knoll, stating they wished to surrender. They stood up waving their empty hands in the air.

"¡Manos arriba!" Hugo ordered again over the loudspeaker as the cartel gunmen slowly emerged with their hands in the air. Hugo continued directing the gunmen to face away from them and to lay face-down on the ground and not move as the teams approached.

The two figures at the top of the knoll, near the spotters shack that Donna hit lay lifeless, and there was a small fire burning behind the yellow stock truck where the RPG landed.

"Javier, Javier, Hugo calling," Hugo shouted over the portable radio.

"Go ahead, Hugo," Captain Javier Fuerte responded.

"Do you see the white Suburban?" Hugo asked.

"No, we took some fire from that direction when we approached and we returned fire, but we have not seen the white Suburban," Captain Fuerte responded.

"Move in slowly, stay alert and we will do the same," Hugo advised.

Both teams moved their vehicles closer to the knoll, closer to the two black Suburbans and the yellow truck, using the navy vehicles for cover. Donna made her way alone on foot, using shrubs and a Boojum Tree for cover, to the top of the knoll and the two men she killed. While the team was checking the surrendered and dead cartel members, Snake and Joe climbed the hill to the shack where they saw Donna bent over one of the dead cartel gunmen.

"What is she doing?" Joe asked.

"You don't want to know," Snake responded as they saw Donna cutting off the little finger of a man's right hand. She put the dismembered finger in her pocket, left the dead men, and approached Joe and Snake. Neither man mentioned to her what they saw.

"I hoped this would not be here," Snake said as he looked inside the shack.

25.

VESTIBULE OF HADES

*A*bandon all hope, ye who enter here. (Henry Francis Cary, The Devine Comedy of Dante), entered Joe's mind as he looked at the nuclear artillery shell.

"It looks like an artillery shell about 34 inches long and 7 inches in diameter. It has a black box attached to it with what appears to be an antenna protruding from the top of the box. I need to get a closer look," Snake said.

"We need to issue the evacuation alert," Joe advised.

"There appears to be a live nuclear artillery shell here modified as an improvised explosive device. Please pass the word to the team to not use their radios until we are a good distance away from this IED," Joe continued.

"I will issue the command for an alert to be dispersed," Captain Fuerte responded.

"What do we do now?" Donna asked no one in particular.

"Let's gather up the weapons, evidence, bodies, our gear and prisoners and head back to the Tijuana Navy Airbase," Marty stated.

"Prisoners?" Joe asked.

"Yes, we have two men, a Russian male and a cartel gunman. We also have seized and impounded 4 nuclear artillery shells," Marty responded.

"Cocaine?" Donna asked as she checked the vehicles.

"None found. The white Suburban did not arrive. The cocaine might be in the white Suburban, but it has disappeared," Captain Fuerte said.

"OK, Snake. Let's get going back to the navy airbase. Since this windstorm seems to be winding down, the helos with the SEALs and Veronica should be arriving soon," Joe advised.

"Tell Veronica... tell Veronica I will see her in a while. I'm staying here to see if I can disarm this thing. When the EOD guys arrive, will you ask them if they would make a Faraday cage and bring it out here to me, something large enough to cover this whole bomb and antenna and allow enough room inside for me to work on this gizmo?" Snake asked.

"Why don't you take some measurements and come back with us and start making that, what do you call it... a Faraday cage?" Joe asked.

"The Faraday cage is a long shot. It will stop radio signals from entering or exiting this device. I want to stay and study the IED part of this contraption and see if there may be a way to defuse it while waiting on the Faraday cage. Send an EOD guy with the cage as soon as possible," Snake requested.

"OK, Snake, I don't like leaving you here, but it sounds reasonable. You need to walk away from this alive and well so that Veronica can continue to admire your scars, my friend. I am leaving this M-14 rifle with you, an extra clip, and some RPG's," Joe said.

"Thanks, Joe," Snake responded, smiling as Joe walked down the hill to the team.

Snake remained in the spotters shack with a flashlight, a book of schematics that translated the details from Russian to English, and a few tools.

What does "vooruzhennyy" and "razoruzhen" in Russian mean? Snake thought to himself. *This IED has a black box that flashes the Russian word "vooruzhennyy" where the other nuclear devices in the truck had black boxes that flashed the word "razoruzhen" on them.* In checking the translation in the schematics book Snake found the IED in the shack was flashing the word "armed" in Russian, and the other IED's that were seized by the team, were flashing the Russian word "disarmed".

All I have to do is get this IED to start flashing disarmed. I wonder why I'm hearing all those sirens off in the distance? Snake thought to himself. He then realized the sirens were alerting citizens to evacuate the area in the event the nuclear device detonated. Sweat began beading on Snake's face as he continued to read the schematics in Russian with translations in English, while rest of the team evacuated the area and headed back to Tijuana.

Upon arrival at the Tijuana Mexican Navy Airbase Joe noticed two unmarked UH-1 Iroquois helicopters parked on the tarmac near the headquarters building.

"Are those the SEAL's Hueys?" Joe asked.

"They must have arrived while we were away," Hugo remarked.

Let's take these prisoners to my office and leave the handcuffs on them and post a guard until we can interrogate them," Captain Fuerte suggested.

Joe, Marty and Hugo made contact with the two SEAL teams and Lieutenant Veronica in the cafeteria.

"Who are your EOD soldiers?" Joe asked a SEAL team member.

"Hank and Frank. That's them over there," the sailor responded, pointing in their direction.

"Gentlemen, my name is Joe Creed, and I just returned from what looks like a nuclear artillery shell modified as an improvised explosive device. We left behind a retired Army Ranger with the IED to study it and attempt to determine how to defuse it," Joe explained.

"Yes, sir, my name is Hank, this is Frank, and we are

prepared to defuse the device. We have studied the details about the Russian 240-millimeter artillery shell and improvised arming methods. Is that what we are dealing with?"

"I think so. I was requested to ask if you would build a Faraday cage large enough for the device and enough room inside the cage for someone to be able to move around and work defusing it," Joe responded.

"We will get right on it. Who do we talk to about the supplies and tools we will need to build the cage?" Frank asked.

"Captain Javier Fuerte. I will find him and get back to you directly," Joe said as he left the room looking for Captain Fuerte.

Joe found Captain Fuerte in his office with the two handcuffed prisoners. Captain Hugo Chávez and Lieutenant Veronica Sabroso were involved in what appeared to be a heated discussion just outside Captain Fuerte's office.

"I will go now," Lieutenant Veronica demanded, glaring at Captain Hugo as Captain Fuerte stood by.

"You will not! I will not risk any more lives than is absolutely necessary," Captain Hugo responded.

A heated dialogue continued in Spanish between Lieutenant Veronica and Captain Hugo, her superior officer, after which she saluted, turned on her heels, and walked away.

"Sorry to interrupt. The EOD guys are looking to build a Faraday cage and need supplies and tools," Joe said to Captain Fuerte.

"I will assist them immediately and leave the interrogation of the Russian and sicario to you, Hugo and Casey," Captain Fuerte responded.

"Thank you, Captain, as they are eager to get that cage to Snake as soon as possible. Captain Hugo, Casey and I will separate the Russian and the cartel gunman and interrogate them," Joe said.

"I can take the cartel gunman into the office across the hall and interrogate him one on one in Spanish," Hugo advised.

"Good, Joe and I will speak with the Russian," Casey responded.

The men went to the respective offices, closed the doors, and proceeded to interrogate the prisoners.

"Tell me about yourself," Casey said while looking the middle aged, portly Russian gentleman in the eye.

"I have the right to remain silent," the Russian responded.

"What do you mean?" Casey asked.

The Russian was silent, so Casey asked again, "What do you mean?"

The Russian stared directly ahead, gritted his teeth, crossed his arms over his chest and said nothing.

"You might be referring to 'Miranda' which is US case law. You only have the right to remain silent while you are in the United States. You are in México now and subject to their laws. I cannot guarantee what will happen to you if I tell the Mexicans that you refuse to speak with us. Things could get very difficult for you," Joe said.

"You speak good English. Where did you study English?" Casey asked.

"I studied meteorology and English at the University of Chicago," the Russian responded.

"I am Joe, and this is Casey. What is your name?" Joe asked.

"I am Igor Khruschev."

"Igor is my middle name. My ancestors came from Russia," Casey declared.

"Your name is Igor also? I do not believe you. This is an interrogation tactic, no? If you are speaking the truth, you will know the meaning of the name Igor in Russian. Otherwise, you are a liar, sir!"

"Warrior. Our name means warrior," Casey responded quietly.

Igor stared at Casey and Joe for a moment, mumbling something in Russian.

"What would you like us to do for you?" Joe asked.

"I do not want to go back to Russia. I want to live in the United States and I will need protection from the Russian KGB," Igor announced.

"I have the authority to make that happen Igor, but you must prove to be of great assistance to the people of the United States," Casey advised.

"Do you have anything worthwhile to tell us?" Joe asked.

"Yes, but will you help me if I help you?" Igor asked.

"Yes. I will do everything I can to help you if what you have to say is worthwhile," Casey responded.

"Ok, *da*. I will trust you. I will tell you what I know about this fanatic Escobar. It is my job to forecast the weather because the wind direction is very important to the plans Escobar has to control the border here. The nuclear devices you have taken were going to be used to make invisible wall at the border so no one could cross under penalty of death from radiation poisoning. The modified nuclear shell in the shack was armed by simply pushing a button. It can only be disarmed by a special radio signal from a transmitter that was carried by Señor Escobar and Pavel, a Russian scientist," Igor disclosed.

"Where is Pavel and Señor Escobar at this moment?" Joe asked.

"Pavel was killed. Two armed guards with Pavel were also killed when we were attacked about 5 kilometers from the first deployment location. The yellow truck was allowed to continue but the white Suburban with Señor Escobar was taken by those who attacked us."

"Who attacked you?" Casey asked.

"I do not know. They were not the police since they wore regular clothes. I suspect they were a rival gang. One of the men was called Pulpo, or something like that."

"Describe Señor Escobar to me," Joe asked.

"Señor Pedro Escobar claims to be Pablo Escobar's

brother, but it is not so. He is not Latino; he is Caucasian and probably American from the USA by the way he talks. At one point during our trip here I overheard Pedro telling Pavel that his real name was Truman, and he was connected with the Bonanno Family from New York City."

Truman is dead, and this jerk is playing games with us. I wonder how he even knows anything about Karter Truman, Joe thought.

"What happened to the white Suburban?" Joe asked.

"Pedro Escobar left with the cartel men driving the white Suburban. They went back, eastbound on Highway 2."

Captain Hugo stepped out of the office where he had been interrogating the cartel gunman and spoke a few words to one of the sailors. The sailor left and returned a few minutes later with Lieutenant Veronica and EOD specialist Hank.

"Do you still wish to see Señor Snake?" Hugo asked Lieutenant Veronica

"Yes, sir, I do."

"You may go with the EOD men who will be taking the Faraday cage to Snake and assist them, but I want your promise you will return here with them."

"Yes, sir, I promise. Thank you very much, Captain. You have a good heart, sir and I appreciate you."

"Do you understand the order I have given Lieutenant Veronica, Señor Hank?"

"Yes, sir. We will be delivering the Faraday cage and will help Snake install it. We will then return here with your Lieutenant, sir," Hank said.

Hank, Frank, and Lieutenant Veronica loaded the Faraday cage into the back of a navy pickup along with some tools. Two Mexican sailors, armed with rifles, rode in the back of the pickup with Hank in the front seat and Lieutenant Veronica driving. A second navy pickup, leading the way, was driven by a sailor with Frank in front and two more armed sailors in the back. Upon arrival, Hank, Frank and Lieutenant Veronica carried the parts of the Faraday cage up the hill to the spotters shack, while the navy sailors took cover and provided protection for the team.

"Veronica! I can't believe it's you," Snake exclaimed with a big smile on his face.

"I cannot stay away from you, *mi serpiente amorosa.*"

"Why are you here? You should not be here. Give me a hug and promise me you will return to the base."

"I am here because of you, and I am under orders to return with the EOD specialists."

"You are named after Saint Veronica who wiped Jesus' face with her veil as He was on his way to crucifixion. You are a great comfort to me, but you must return, my love. I want to defuse this monster before it goes off. I need to speak with the EOD specialists for a few minutes before you leave."

"Yes, speak with them now, then disarm this thing and promise to return to me at the airbase."

"That is my intention my love, to return to you, but I do not know what God intends," Snake said, looking deep into Lieutenant Veronica's eyes, as he reached out and touched a teardrop on her cheek.

After assembling the Faraday cage, which hopefully will block the nuclear device from receiving radio signals and stop the improvised detonator from being activated by a remote transmitter, Snake, Hank, and Frank went over the schematics and detailed information about the device. They spent twenty minutes reviewing several options.

"It's time to go," Hank reported as the men began walking down the hill to the pickups.

"Here are the keys to the second pickup, Snake, just in case you need to get out of here quickly. When you get that thing defused, give us a call on your portable radio. We will have the Mexican sailors take custody of it. They already have the other four disarmed nukes," Frank said.

"Veronica, would you do me a favor?" Snake asked.

"Anything, *mi amor.*"

"Take this patch and put it up on the bulletin board in the cafeteria at the base next to the patches from other visiting military soldiers. I forgot to do that earlier," Snake said as he handed her a uniform patch worn by tunnel rats in Vietnam.

"I will do as you ask as I await your return with an aching heart," Veronica whispered as she removed her scarf and wiped Snake's face.

Snake stood in the open doorway of the shack and watched as the team withdrew. Lieutenant Veronica sobbed quietly to herself as she drove away.

26.

Baja Burning

The team arrived back at the airbase just as the rising sun produced a faint glow in the eastern sky. Lieutenant Veronica removed the tunnel rats patch from her pocket that Snake gave her. It was oval in shape, about three inches in diameter with a cartoon rat in the center of the patch holding a pistol and a flashlight. The words "Tunnel Rat" was embroidered over the top of the patch and the Latin words, "Non Gratum Anus Rodentum" across the bottom. She stared at it for a long time, until Hugo approached.

"How is Snake doing?" Hugo asked.

"He is working on the IED, but it is difficult, and he is not sure how long it will take. He will notify us by radio when he has it defused."

"How are you doing?"

"I am worried for… all the people in this area, including the team and especially Snake. I will be glad when this is over and the biggest worry we may have is how to rescue stranded fishermen."

"I agree." Hugo remarked.

Lieutenant Veronica stepped outside into the early morning air to think and clear her head. She thought of the local families, the poor and salt of the earth. They had to pack up their belongings and leave in the early morning hours, as the sirens continued to shriek into the chilled night air. They had to leave behind their livestock, pets, home, and outbuildings to a possible nuclear explosion which would incinerate everything the families had worked so hard for. She thought of parents who had to worry about survival of their children in this new atomic age, which they had little knowledge of. They may have seen the photos of what happened in Hiroshima and Nagasaki, and they were terrified it could happen to them. She thought of Snake, a man she admired beyond description, and whom she had fallen in love with, working alone on the hideous atomic device. She wished she could be next to him, providing him with a tender devotion and admiring his courage as a warrior.

Then it happened.

She saw a double flash lighting up the eastern sky with a hot, blinding, white light, that immediately ignited fires in the tinder dry desert, followed about 20 seconds later with a blast wave from the explosion that leveled structures within a mile of the hypocenter and immediately blew out some of the fires started by the heat from the blast. She put her hands in front of her eyes to shield them and saw the flesh become transparent, displaying all the bones in her hands, a result of the X-rays from the nuclear explosion. She became almost immediately catatonic and horrified with fear, riveted in place.

Even though everyone had prepared for this possible moment in their minds, the actual event shocked and frightened everyone to their core. Some stood frozen, looking to the east at the mushroom cloud rising in the early morning sky, with blank looks on their faces.

"Are you OK? Have you been burned? Are your eyes, OK?" Joe asked quickly seeing Lieutenant Veronica was in distress.

"Did you see it?" she asked.

"No, I was inside when it happened. I see the mushroom

cloud rising in the air. What did you see?" Joe asked.

"I saw Snake's face in the mushroom cloud smiling at me," she said with tears rolling down her cheeks.

"You didn't see it? Snake is now truly part of our environment," she said while holding her face in her hands.

"Are you OK?" Joe asked.

"I am blind. I cannot see a thing. I feel like death."

"Here, take my arm. I will lead you to the base infirmary."

The roar of the explosion slowly subsided while the mushroom cloud continued to climb into the atmosphere. Many radios, the electric grid, and most electronic components were damaged by the large electronic pulse created by the blast. The sirens stopped, and it was deathly quiet as the sun, behind the mushroom cloud, began to rise throwing shadows on the landscape and illuminating the ominous cloud.

Damage was minimal to the Mexican Navy Airbase at Tijuana, and at the base infirmary people were beginning to arrive with injuries ranging from light sunburns to third degree burns, blunt force trauma, blindness, and hysteria. The SEAL team members and others, trained in first aid, reported to the base infirmary to assist with injured patients.

"Take a look at this guy," Hank said to Joe.

The shirtless man turned his back to Joe. There were second degree burns on his back formed in the words "Coyote Auto Parts". The rest of the skin on his back was normal.

"I will bet this man was wearing a light-colored shirt with the words "Coyote Auto Parts" written on the back of his shirt in dark letters," Joe observed.

"OK, I think I understand. This man had his back turned when the blast went off and the light-colored shirt reflected the radiation, but the dark letters absorbed the thermal radiation, causing his burns, right?" Hank replied.

"That's my guess, strange huh?"

After patients stopped coming to the infirmary, Captain Fuerte assembled 4 trauma response teams comprised of

Mexican medical personnel, assisted by SEAL team members, to travel out to the areas where they were needed on both sides of the border. Each SEAL team member carried a dosimeter which measured the amount of radiation exposure, and they were ordered to report back to the base when each had reached a maximum dosage. Most portable radios, which had been switched off during the explosion, continued to operate. Civil defense teams on both sides of the border were activated and dispatched to aid and evacuate the injured.

The next day EOD team members Hank and Frank remained at the airbase to turn over the four remaining nuclear artillery shells to the Mexican Navy explosive ordinance disposal counterpart, for shipment to a remote Mexican storage depot. The mushroom cloud had disappeared, and the sun rose with a beautiful sunrise of different shades of red playing across the clouds in the eastern sky. Casey and Captain Fuerte called for a general meeting of all personnel at the airbase hangar to determine priorities, needs and mission plans. Telephone service was intermittent but beginning to return to normal. Calls were coming in from the news media world-wide. After roll call, it was agreed that the first priority of the team was aid to the injured and ill. Assistance for the displaced families and aid in locating missing persons was also discussed as high priority missions. Outlining the nuclear hot zone was considered a high priority also. It was determined that a helicopter would be used to take radiation measurements with a Geiger counter. A team of two sailors in a vehicle on the ground, also outfitted with a Geiger counter, took measurements and posted warning signs around the perimeter of the high radiation area in coordination with the helicopter.

"The size and shape of the high radiation zone would be determined by the strength and direction of the winds at the time of the explosion," Casey noted as the ground and air teams made preparations to map the hot zone.

"Casey, there is a telephone call for you," Hugo reported.

A few moments later Casey returned and declared, "That was the director. He will be calling back with the President of the United States on the line in 30 minutes. He wants all of us to listen on the speaker phone and be ready to respond to any questions the president may have.

Casey, Captain Fuerte, Hugo, Donna, Joe, Marty, Veronica, Hank and Frank from the SEAL teams all gathered in Captain Fuerte's office. Veronica was wearing sunglasses due to eye damage from the nuclear blast. Her sight was slowly returning to normal. Joe and Marty checked the connections on the STU phone while they waited for the call from the president. The phone rang.

"Hello, this is Casey."

"Hi Casey, this is Bill Colby from the home office."

"Yes, Director Colby. Can you hear me clearly, do we have a good connection?"

"It's a little scratchy on this end, but I can hear you clearly. Mr. President, are you there?"

"Hello, yes. This is President Ford. I can hear you clearly. Luis, can you hear us?"

"Yes, this is Luis Echeverria, the President of México, and I can hear you perfectly."

"Good. This is CIA Director Colby. Casey, would you let the folks on your end introduce themselves and explain which agency they represent?"

"Yes, sir. I am Casey Abbott, with the United States Central Intelligence Agency."

"I am Donna Ashford, with the United States Drug Enforcement Administration."

"I am Captain Javier Fuerte with the Armada de México."

"I am Lieutenant Veronica Sabroso with the Armada de México."

"Hank and Frank, we are EOD specialists with the US Navy SEALs."

"I am Captain Hugo Chávez also with the Armada de México."

"Joe Creed, former law-enforcement, investigator on leave from State Farm Insurance Company."

"Martin Goodson, United States Federal Bureau of Investigation."

"It is a pleasure to meet all nine of you during these terrible circumstances. Would someone kindly provide me with a brief history surrounding the explosion of the nuclear device on our southern border?"

"Yes, sir, I think I can do that," Marty responded. "Investigator Joe Creed and I assembled a team to locate and arrest a wanted law enforcement detective, a federal fugitive from Washington State, that fled to the Mexican Baja Peninsula. While engaged in that mission we learned the CIA and the DEA were conducting a joint mission to stop 5 Russian improvised nuclear explosive devices from being placed and detonated on the border between México and the United States. When our mission was completed, we assisted Casey, with the CIA, and Donna, with the DEA, in their efforts to stop the deployment of the nuclear devices, render them safe, and apprehend the persons involved."

"This is Casey, Mr. President. We have seized 4 of the Russian nuclear devices, disarmed them and turned them over to the Mexican military to be transported to their Sonoran Desert waste disposal and storage facility. We issued an alert on both sides of the border as a precaution prior to the explosion and assisted in the evacuation of civilians. We were unable to disarm the single device that was deployed east of our location, and we lost one very brave man who had been attempting to disarm it when it exploded. We have been aiding the injured and are ready to map out the high radiation area and get it cordoned off."

"Do we have an idea who did this crime?"

"This is Donna Abbot. DEA suspects drug kingpin Pablo

Escobar and his associates are the perpetrators. We do not have all the names and details, but we are working on it."

"Do any of you think nuclear IED's are going to be used in the future?"

"I think this is a rare circumstance, Mr. President. I do not think Russia is voluntarily allowing their nukes to disappear and since 5 have been stolen, I hope Russia will take security of their weapons more seriously," Casey responded.

"We have redoubled our efforts to monitor Russian nuclear arms movements in response to this incident," Director Colby advised.

"There was a cocaine shipment along with the nuclear arms that originated from Columbia, is that correct?" the President asked.

"This is Donna with the DEA, Mr. President. We lost contact with the cocaine shipment and at least two cartel members when we advanced on the location where the first IED had been deployed. The radio transmitter that could have ignited the nuclear explosion may have been with the men who escaped."

"Well, it sounds as if you have your work cut out for you. Is there anything you need or is there anything I can do for you to assist in this mission?"

"Not that I can think of at the moment, Mr. President," Casey responded.

"This is President Echeverria, You have the full support of the Mexican government, and we will assist the team in any way we can."

"Unless there is something else, we will be signing off. Please give our condolences to the family of your lost team member, and you have my support in bringing the situation back to normal as much as possible," President Ford declared.

27.

THE INFERNO

The effects of the nuclear blast continued to make themselves known. The toll of 173 dead and 228 missing continued to rise daily. An area of about 20 miles wide and 200 miles long was designated a hot zone of deadly radiation after a survey was completed by air and ground. It was expected that most of the area would remain a dead zone for at least 5 years. The hypocenter area of the blast was observed from a helicopter during the radiation assessment. The knoll and spotters shack were gone and in its place was a circular hole in the earth about the size of a football field and approximately 30 feet deep. The navy pickup was gone as were all signs of life, leaving only a scorched desert landscape with gleaming bits of a shiny substance surrounding the center of the blast. Downwind from the blast, after the mushroom cloud dissipated, it began raining black drops of rain about the size of marbles for about an hour. The strange black rainstorm, following the horror of the nuclear blast, instilled more fear in those who observed it.

The black rain reminded Joe of Snake's statement of the vision he saw in the tunnels. He reported black ash like substance, from the nuclear blast illusion, covered them and was difficult to wash off.

Captain Fuerte called for a team meeting to assess their missions and determine future activities.

"I call this meeting to order," announced Captain Fuerte as the team gathered in the base cafeteria. An interpreter repeated Captain Fuerte's words in Spanish.

"Who can tell me how the rescue and medical missions are going?" Captain Fuerte asked.

"SEAL teams Bigfoot and Rat Pack both have emergency first aid training and individual members were assigned to accompany and assist the Mexican medical trauma teams aiding civilians on both sides of the border," Casey responded.

"Most of the SEAL team members have received a daily maximum dose of radiation and since calls for rescues or assistance have dropped off, SEAL teams are now on standby mode. Mexican and US Fire Departments are currently responding to calls for aid," Casey continued.

"Can anyone explain the reports of large drops of black rain occurring?" Captain Fuerte asked.

"It is not uncommon after a nuclear blast for black rain to fall. The rain is radioactive and should be avoided. The fallout contains a demons brew of radioactive elements that causes water vapor to form large, dark, droplets of water, falling as black rain, " Casey explained.

"What are the chances for further attacks from the cartels?" Hugo asked.

"My guess is they are all either on the run or are hiding out from expected responses from Mexican and US governments to the nuclear incident," Donna remarked.

"There is one thing I think we should act on as soon as possible. The nuclear attack at the border was planned and executed by the Escobar cartel from Columbia, we believe. We have two members of the Escobar cartel in the base brig now that may be able to provide us with more information about who, what, where, and other important information about the attack. We need to know about the Escobar cartel member that escaped in the white Suburban," Donna continued.

"I notified US law enforcement to be on the lookout for the white suburban with possible Mexican plates driven by a white male adult, but without more information I think the all-points bulletin is a shot in the dark," Marty reported.

"Casey and I spoke with the Russian meteorologist and he is willing to assist us, however, he may not tell us the whole truth. He claims Pedro Escobar, Pablo's brother, is not a Columbian and is not Pablo's brother. He states the man's surname is Truman. Karter Truman, the former prosecutor, who died in an automobile crash a few years ago. If he is saying Pedro Escobar is Karter Truman, he has to be lying," Joe declared.

"If I recall correctly, Karter Truman's business card was found on the sailboat Just Dandy and another business card was found on MV Bass Reeves, both with the San Javier compound phone number written on the back of the cards, including the distinctive number seven with a line through it, just as was Karter Truman's habit, correct?" Marty asked.

"Yes, that is correct. We assumed Nick Cabot left the cards because Truman was killed in a car crash, but then, Truman's body was almost completely consumed in the fire. I suppose it is remotely possible the burned body was not Karter Truman," Joe responded.

"It would be nice if we could identify this character. Can you have a photo of Karter Truman faxed to the navy base here so we can see what the Russian says?" Donna asked.

"I could give Agent Madison Gardner a call to see if she could find a photo of Truman and fax it to us," Marty replied.

"Good, Captain Lloyd spent a lot of time with this Pedro Escobar aboard MV Bass Reeves and he may also be helpful," Joe said.

"I was able to make contact with Buck and Annie at the Loreto airport. They were worried about us. I asked that they make sure Captain Lloyd does not leave and MV Bass Reeves remains impounded until we return. We may need Captain Lloyd to identify Pedro Escobar from a photo," Marty explained.

"Hello, yes, I am trying to reach Special Project Agent Madison Gardner. OK, I'll wait," Marty stated in a telephone call to Washington DC.

"Hello?"

"Madison, is that you?" Marty asked.

"Hi, Marty. Yes, this is Madison. Are you OK?"

"I'm well, Madison. I'm in México with Joe Creed and the team completing a mission. Would you hook up a STU phone for a private conversation?" Marty asked.

"Sure, Marty. Give me a minute."

"OK, there we go. Can you hear me OK?"

"Yes, I can hear you clearly."

"It's good to know you are all OK. What's happening down there in México besides nuclear explosions?"

"Our original mission was to work with the Mexican authorities to arrest former narcotics detective Nick Cabot. That mission has been completed with the unfortunate death of Nick Cabot and his former girlfriend. In response to information from you, we were able to contact agents from the CIA and DEA in order to keep our mission from interfering with each other. We have since assisted the two agencies in an attempt to stop the Escobar cartel from setting off 5 nuclear IED's at the border. As you may have heard, we were not successful in stopping the first nuke from exploding. We also lost Snake in the blast as he was trying to defuse the IED when it detonated, but we confiscated the remaining 4 nukes and are now interested in the people behind this disaster."

"Oh, no. Snake was a very special and unique person. It saddens me to hear of his loss. How can I help, Marty?"

"Would you be willing to contact the sheriff's office in

the county where Snake lived to ask them to notify the family of his death? We also lost track of one of the vehicles and people involved in the nuclear blast incident. He goes by the name of Pedro Escobar, claims to be Pablo Escobar's brother, but is more likely a US citizen instead of a Columbian. He was traveling in a white Chevrolet Suburban with Mexican plates and may be traveling north across the US-Mexican border. We have been receiving information he has alluded to being former Prosecutor Karter Truman who we thought died in a fiery automobile crash."

"May Snake rest in peace. He was one of a kind. I will make sure his family is properly notified. I have a copy of Karter Truman's death certificate in my file, Marty. The reports indicate the body was so destroyed by fire that identifying characteristics were not available. Dental records were not located, so that body may be Karter Truman, or it could be someone else."

"When Officers Joe Creed and Jim Sorenson tried to arrest him and were chasing Karter Truman in his Mercedes sedan, they lost sight of him for a couple moments just before the crash. It is possible Truman got out of the car unseen and survived. If that is the case, I wonder who the corpse belongs to? Is there any chance you can locate a good photo of Truman and fax it to us? We have a couple of people here who may recognize him."

"Absolutely, I'm sure there are some photos of him from the most recent election. I will fax them to you as soon as possible."

"Is this the best phone number to reach you, Madison? I suspect we may need more of your help as we follow up and try to identify and locate this Pedro Escobar or whomever he may be."

"Yes, it is Marty. Feel free to call me anytime. I will get back to you with the photo soon."

28.

WHO IS PEDRO ESCOBAR?

Lieutenant Veronica was walking across the tarmac to a hangar at the Tijuana Mexican Navy Base when she saw a sailor running past her with a shovel in his hand. She watched as he ran up to two other sailors near the hangar who were looking at something on the ground.

"*¿Que paso?*" she asked wanting to know what held their interest.

¡*Serpiente!* the sailor responded while pointing at a large rattlesnake on the ground.

"*Dame la pala,*" Lieutenant Veronica ordered, pointing at the shovel he was holding.

She took the shovel from the sailor and gently slid it under the middle of a large rattlesnake and lifted it up off the ground. The snake coiled peacefully in a circle in the middle of the shovel and looked directly at her with his tongue flicking in and out of his mouth. She smiled and spoke softly in English to the snake as the sailors watched with their jaws hanging open. She lifted the shovel up to her face while continuing to speak softly. The sailors would later swear the rattlesnake was smiling at Lieutenant Veronica as they looked into each other's eyes from a very close distance.

"OK," Lieutenant Veronica replied, as if she was responding to something she heard.

She took the snake in the shovel and walked over to the fence line, put the rattlesnake down on the ground, and watched as it slithered away into the brush.

My heart just aches for mi serpiente, she thought to herself.

She handed the shovel back to the sailor, who noticed she had tears in her eyes as she walked away.

The news media continued to report the nuclear destruction story day after day. A chartered aircraft with a pilot and two television news reporters flew into the restricted area taking video of the destruction. Two hours after they landed and had submitted their reports, the reporters and the pilot began suffering symptoms of radiation poisoning. The media began following the progress of the two reporters and pilot as their symptoms increased.

Classic radiation poisoning symptoms included vomiting, diarrhea, headache, fever, internal bleeding, hair loss and a difficult death. The media story shifted from the destruction of the Baja to the step by horrifying step, of death by radiation poisoning of the two reporters and pilot.

Foo Fighters were seen circling clockwise about 3000 feet above a Mexican navy truck in the early morning as it transported the 4 nuclear IED's to a Mexican nuclear waste storage facility in the Sonoran Desert. The Foo Fighters followed the truck into the distance and then disappeared.

Captain Fuerte called for a team meeting and reported he had telephone contact with cartel Lieutenant Pulpo who was willing to provide him with what he knows about the white Suburban and the man who calls himself Pedro Escobar.

"Pulpo wants to meet us at Chico's Cantina in Pueblo Maritza again. He says he has information for us about Pedro Escobar," Captain Fuerte advised.

"Is that area safe from radiation?" Donna asked.

"It suffered some destruction, but the radiation levels are low enough we can spend an hour in the area without causing us problems," Captain Fuerte responded.

"Even though we don't trust this guy, we need to hear what he has to say," Joe remarked.

"We also need to understand why he wants to provide us with information as it must benefit him somehow, I suspect," Donna commented.

The photograph of Karter Truman arrived by fax at Captain Fuerte's office. Copies were made and provided to Captain Hugo Chávez and Lieutenant Veronica Sabroso. Casey made arrangements for Hugo and Veronica to be flown by one of the SEAL helicopters back to Puerto Escondido where they planned to contact Captain Lloyd, to get his response to the photo.

Casey and Joe took a photo of Karter Truman and made contact at the brig with the Russian meteorologist.

"I'm Joe and this is Casey. What is your name?" Joe asked after they were let into the holding cell.

"I told you before I am Igor Khrushchev."

"You agreed to speak honestly with us earlier, is that correct?" Joe asked.

"Yes, sir. What would you like to know?" he asked revealing a slight Russian accent.

Casey handed Khrushchev the photo of Karter Truman and asked, "Have you ever seen this man?"

"Yes, that is Pedro Escobar. I spent much time with him on this crazy project."

"Tell me about him," Joe inquired with Casey listening.

"Family, family, family, that is all he would talk about. He is not a Columbian, and his Columbian passport is counterfeit. He said he was a member of the Bonanno family from New York."

"I asked him if he wanted me to call him Pedro, like everybody else, and he said Pedro was OK, but his real name was Karter. He didn't like people asking him personal questions too much, so we did not talk about that again. Can you tell me what is going to happen to me?"

"México does not have the death penalty, so unless you get extradited to the United States, you will probably live to spend the rest of your life incarcerated, but that will be up to the Mexican justice system," Casey responded.

"Your cooperation will be noted, and we can ask the Mexican judge to give you some leniency, depending on the quality and amount of assistance you provide. You will probably be asked to give a recorded deposition by Mexican investigators and lawyers. Cooperating with them would be to your benefit," Joe advised before they left.

"How can it be? Is Karter Truman alive or has someone taken his identity?" Joe asked.

"What advantage would it give someone to impersonate Karter Truman?" Casey responded.

"None. There is a quashed federal warrant for Karter Truman who is officially deceased. I cannot understand how it would benefit anyone to take his name," Joe answered.

"It could be Karter Truman himself," Casey proposed just as Captain Fuerte approached them.

"Joe, I asked the cartel gunman we are holding if he would agree to cooperate by looking at a photo and he spit on my shoes. You have a call from Captain Hugo at Puerto Escondido and you can take it in my office."

Joe, Casey and Captain Fuerte went to Captain Fuerte's office for the holding phone call.

"Hello, this is Joe, Casey and Captain Fuerte here on the speaker phone. Is that you, Hugo?" Joe asked.

"Yes, it is. Greetings everyone. I have a report for you about the photo we showed to Captain Lloyd of the cargo ship Bass Reeves. He swears the photo is that of a man who boarded his ship off the coast of Columbia near the town of Buenaventura calling himself Pedro Escobar. He further states he believes the man is not Columbian, he appears to be a US citizen in the way he talks and things he told them.

He has provided us with a signed deposition stating the same. He has also agreed to testify, if called, and is asking us to release him, his crew and MV Bass Reeves, so that he may deliver the load of fertilizer to the farming cooperative in Guaymas. Captain Lloyd showed us the cabin occupied by Pedro Escobar during the voyage and we have recovered some latent fingerprints to be compared with those of your deceased prosecutor, if you have them."

"That is excellent, Hugo. Fingerprints may give us the answer. Would you make copies and send us the originals?" Marty asked.

"Yes, of course. I will send the original latent prints back with the SEAL helicopter when it returns to the Tijuana Navy Base."

"I can't see any reason to further detain Captain Lloyd, unless someone else thinks we should hold him," Joe remarked.

It was agreed to release Captain Lloyd, his crew, and MV Bass Reeves to complete their voyage to Guaymas, México to deliver the load of fertilizer, provided that Captain Lloyd agreed to keep in contact with Captain Hugo weekly for the next 6 months.

Captain Fuerte, Joe, Marty, and Donna were all armed with concealed Colt .45 caliber pistols, along with 4 sailors armed with M-14 rifles. They took two navy pickups for a noon meeting with cartel lieutenant Pulpo at Chico's Cantina in the tiny settlement of Pueblo Maritza. The 30-minute drive east of Tijuana traveled outside the radiation exclusion zone, but still well within the area of blast destruction. Palm trees and telephone poles were all leaning the same direction or completely toppled over. Farm animals that were still alive were loose and wandering around dazed and sick looking. Many small, impoverished looking farm homes and outbuildings were knocked down and appeared abandoned. A whiff of decomposing flesh was noticed occasionally as they continued driving east.

"I hope they all got out of here before the blast," Donna said as they passed another abandoned farm.

"I would like to approach Chico's Cantina cautiously. I think we should leave one pickup about 100 meters from the cantina while the other one parks near the front door with armed sailors in both vehicles. I do not trust this Pulpo at all," Captain Fuerte declared.

Chico's Cantina and the small Pueblo Maritza settlement suffered blast and thermal damage. The painted sign on the north wall of the cantina was scorched and peeling. The building itself had been moved a few inches off its foundation and the windows were boarded up, except for the front window, which was missing. The dusty streets were vacant except for a tall Mexican cowboy leaning against a wall, wearing a large sombrero, cowboy boots, and a multicolored tilma or cloak.

"That guy could be packing," Joe cautioned as they entered the pueblo slowly.

"Stay alert," Captain Fuerte ordered.

"Stay apart and keep your eyes peeled," Joe remarked.

The navy pickup with two Mexican sailors parked at the end of the block and kept a lookout for the team, while the second navy pickup parked in front of Chico's Cantina. Joe, Marty, Donna and Captain Fuerte walked in the front door of the cantina. The thin female was not pole dancing this time, and there were no other customers in the cantina. There was same bartender, about 50 years old, wearing a stained white T-shirt, cowboy boots and jeans. He approached the table.

"*Bienvenidos. ¿Qué quieres?,*" the bartender asked.

"He's asking what you want." Captain Fuerte translated.

"*Tiene te helado en la botella?*" Donna asked.

"*¿Si, y otra?*"

"You guys want beer?" Captain Fuerte asked.

"OK, 3 beers and a bottle of iced tea," Captain Fuerte

responded. Then again in Spanish.

Joe noticed the large square table where they sat had a heavy metal top that was stained and dented. The open window allowed more light into the cantina this time and he could see some of the dents in the tabletop appeared to be from bullets. Some small round holes had been repaired with what looked like bondo which is used in automotive body and fender repair work. A closer look at the wood floor of the cantina under the table revealed black stains in the shape of liquid pools that had since dried. Joe noticed Donna was looking at the floor while Casey and Captain Fuerte were carrying on a conversation. Pulpo made a grand entrance from a doorway behind the bar. A cartel *sicario* also came out and stood guard behind the bar, watching Joe, Donna, Casey, and Captain Fuerte. Pulpo was wearing a loose fitting, shimmering blue satin jumpsuit that had high collars turned up. He approached the table smiling and reached out to shake hands. Donna was the last to shake hands with Pulpo and as she did so, she held his hand and instead of shaking it she pulled his hand up to her face and looked closely at his fingers. Then she turned his hand over and stared directly at his little finger. Tension began to rise the longer she held his hand and looked at it. Pulpo was able to pull his hand free and both Pulpo and Donna straightened up as she said, "Sorry, you have such nice hands. I admire nice looking men's hands."

"*No problema, chica*. We can talk about it later," Pulpo responded with a seductive smile.

"Yes, I hope so," Donna responded as she gave him a flirty look.

"So, tell me. Who are you guys, anyway? I know Captain Fuerte is a sailor with Armada de México, but who do you gringos work for, CIA, FBI, DEA, right?"

"We came here to speak with you about the people in the white Suburban because you agreed to talk to us. Is that not so?" Captain Fuerte asked.

"Yea, right. But I want to know who I am talking to, *Capitán*."

Donna continued to look down at the floor, while the conversation proceeded. Then, without notice she stood up, pulled her Colt .45 caliber pistol, pointed it at Pulpo's chest, and pulled the trigger twice. The impacts of the bullets caused his chair to scoot backwards and, while he was still moving, she shot him once again in the forehead. The force of the headshot caused him to topple over backwards, dead, onto the dirty old blood-stained floor.

The gunshots stunned everyone. The cartel gunman behind the bar was Donna's immediate second target. Just as his hand came up with a pistol in it, her 4th round hit him right at the tip of his nose, exploding his head and causing pieces of him to shower in all directions. The bartender ducked down and disappeared. Joe, Casey and Captain Fuerte drew their weapons and backed up to the front door of the cantina and waited while Joe looked outside. Donna was under the table next to Pulpo's body.

She looked up and thought, *when people have a near death experience, they say they can look down upon their body. I wonder if his spirit is looking down on his dead ass right now?* Instead she saw a cockroach nibbling on a small red piece of Pulpo's brain matter sticking to the cantina ceiling.

The navy pickups were running and ready to go. Several armed cartel men came running down the street in their direction. *Wham!* A bullet hit the tailgate of the navy pickup as Casey, Donna, Joe and Captain Fuerte jumped aboard. The sailors in the navy pickup at the end of the block began returning fire at the group of armed men, causing them to scatter, and allowing the team to flee quickly out of Pueblo Maritza.

"Please check yourselves for any injuries. The bullets were flying back there, and I want to make sure no one was hit," Joe stated.

"You have blood on your pants," Casey pointed out to Donna.

"I'm OK. It's someone else's blood," she said as she touched the lump her pocket.

"Donna, would you tell us why you jumped up, out of the blue, pulled your pistol and shot Pulpo?" Casey asked.

While smiling, Donna reached around to her back pocket and pulled out a small mirror and showed it to everyone.

"I need this mirror to check my makeup. I also need it to keep an eye out under cantina tables for dangerous things that could hurt us, like in the case today. Pulpo had a pistol pointed at your *huevos,* Casey, and since he was pulling the hammer back, I decided it was time to stop him, so I shot him. You're welcome."

"I had no idea Donna, thank you."

"No problem. Here is his pistol," she said as she pulled a Smith and Wesson model 19 .357 magnum, fully loaded pistol, from her waistband.

"He had a death grip on the revolver, but I got it out of his hand with a little work," Donna said with a wicked grin on her face.

Back at the Tijuana Naval Airbase Captain Fuerte asked Joe, Casey and Donna to each write reports on the incident at Pueblo Maritza and Chico's Cantina.

The SEAL helicopter arrived from Puerto Escondido with latent fingerprints taken from Pedro Escobar's cabin on MV Bass Reeves. Marty contacted Agent Madison Gardner at the FBI headquarters in Washington DC by telephone.

"Madison, is that you?" Marty asked.

"Hi, Marty. It is good to hear your voice. Do you want me to connect the STU phone?"

"Yes, please. I will do the same now on my end."

"There we go. Can you hear me OK, Marty?"

"Yes, there is a little echo, but I can understand you well enough."

"Are you guys all OK? You sure have a way of getting everyone's attention."

"We are all fine except Snake, as I told you earlier."

"I was able to contact Snake's family and let them know about his death. They were shocked and saddened to hear the news. I offered condolences from all of us."

"Thank you, Madison, for notifying Snake's family. He is sorely missed by those of us who have depended on his expertise. He was a man of great honor and courage and I wish he was still with us."

"His family is planning services at a later date. They promised to notify us of the time and place."

"Good, I'm looking forward to the service, Madison. We have some latent prints here taken from a cabin on the Bass Reeves that may answer our question about the true identity of Pedro Escobar. I'm wondering if we have Karter Truman's prints on file for a comparison?"

"I will find out, Marty. You may not need to send the prints to me for a comparison if you have someone there that can classify fingerprints."

"That's a good idea. I will check and get back to you. Meanwhile I will make a copy of the latent prints we have and get the originals to you."

"OK, Marty. I will call you back if I find a copy of Truman's prints on file."

Joe saw Donna in the cafeteria's kitchen next to a pot of something simmering. He wanted to know her thoughts on what happened to Pedro Escobar and the 250 kilos of cocaine.

"Hey, Donna, what's cooking?" Joe asked as he approached.

"Nothing much, just getting something cleaned up."

"I'd like to get your thoughts on where we're at with Pedro Escobar and the shipment of cocaine."

"It's gone. So is Pedro Escobar, or whomever he might be. What I'm hearing is that the Escobar cartel in Columbia has made a direct connection with the Bonanno mob family of New York City. Escobar is the wholesaler and Bonanno is the retailer of one of the most profitable, illegal enterprises ever in the history of mankind. Our chances of causing them to even skip a beat is almost impossible. It would not surprise me if our government becomes even more corrupt and turns totally to the dark side. This nuclear incident at the border, even though it was not a total success, shows the competing cartels and governments who is in charge and that it would be to their benefit to join with the Escobar cartel, or at least accede to their demands. The combined and coordinated efforts of the Escobar cartel and the Bonanno mob is a major challenge to both governments and the people of México and the United States. I just hope we are up to the challenge."

"That does not paint a very good picture for the future, Donna. What do you think needs to be done?"

"First, both governments need to commission a secret task force to work in an open and honest relationship with each other, with the singular goal of dismantling both criminal enterprises. If that can be achieved, we have a chance of stopping the corruption."

A sailor appeared in the doorway asking, "Señor Joe ? You have a telephone call waiting in the Capitan's Oficina."

"Thanks for your time, Donna. It looks like I better answer this call. Good luck with whatever you're cooking there."

"Thanks," Donna responded with a smile.

"This call is for you, Joe. I will be in the cafeteria if you need me," Captain Fuerte advised as he handed the receiver to Joe.

"Hi, Joe, this is Ed Rust with State Farm Insurance Company. How are you doing, are you OK?"

"Yes, sir. I'm fine. I didn't expect a call from my CEO, sir. How may I help you?"

"The work you have been engaged in with the Mexican and United States governments has made me proud that

State Farm has been able to assist in the protection of citizens on both sides of the border. We all are very proud of you Joe. I took the liberty of calling your wife, Lydia, to let her know the value of the work you've been performing. She said you have been away too long and wanted to know when you would be returning home. I was not able to give her a definite answer, but she understands the importance of your work. She would love to have a long, leisurely, vacation with you for maybe a trip to Malta, when your mission is completed. She said she has many cousins in Malta. I told her I plan on promoting you to vice president of operations for México, Central, and South America which would double your yearly salary. What do you think of that, Joe?"

"Thank you very much, sir. I appreciate your support and encouragement. I'm not sure what is going to happen next."

"I can tell you, Joe, but please keep it to yourself, because there will be no official announcement. President Ford and President Echeverria have agreed to form a secret task force of highly trusted individuals from both countries to investigate the recent events, in order to aggressively counter the organized criminals. Their goal is total annihilation of the criminal gangs that perpetrated the nuclear explosion. You, Joe, will be part of the secret task force with the unpublicized blessing of State Farm Insurance."

"From all the evidence and indications I have observed, sir, the secret task force of trusted members from both countries is exactly what is needed. I would be honored to serve."

"Great. I will let you get back to work. Please know you have my full support. Call me if you need anything. God be with you, Joe."

The sound of a helicopter landing at the Tijuana Navy Airbase suggested to Joe that the SEAL helicopter had returned from Puerto Escondido. A few minutes later, SEAL and EOD Specialist Hank showed up at Captain Fuerte's office doorway.

"Greetings, gentlemen. I have something important for you," Hank announced as he held out a sealed manila envelope to Joe.

"Please put your initials, the date and time on the envelope and I will do the same in order to maintain a record of the chain of custody," Hank requested.

Joe did as he was asked and then took custody of the large envelope. He opened it and took out 6 white paper cards. Each had black fingerprint patterns on the white paper cards, covered with clear plastic tape. Four appeared to be almost complete fingerprints and the other two were clearly visible like the first four, but they were only a partial fingerprint.

"Thank you, Hank. I now need to find somebody who is familiar with the method of classifying fingerprints," Joe stated.

"Good luck with that, sir. Team Bigfoot and team Rat Pack will be standing by if you need us again, sir."

"Thank your team for me, Hank. This is a big help to the cause," Joe stated as his mind turned to classifying the latent fingerprints.

The fax machine in Captain Fuerte's office began warming up, and at the same moment the telephone rang.

"It's for you, Joe," Captain Fuerte stated.

"Hi, Joe, how are you doing? This is Madison in Washington DC."

"I'm doing well Madison. How may I help you?"

"Just an update, do you want to use the STU phone?"

"No, not if it's just a quick update."

"OK, I just sent you a fax with Karter Truman's National Crime Information Center fingerprint card and classification. I was pretty sure we would find a copy of Truman's fingerprints since we insist on having prints of all law enforcement officers and military personnel. They should be coming through to you soon."

"I'm getting them now, Madison. I will mount the 6 latent prints we have and send copies of them via fax to you. Hopefully someone will be able to verify or eliminate a match with Karter Truman. I will take a look myself, but I learned the Henry method in the academy, and I understand it is quite different from the NCIC method you now use."

"You are correct, Joe. Why don't we just wait for an official confirmation from our fingerprint section?"

"I agree Madison. I will hold these originals in the case file."

"OK, Joe. Would you please update Marty to our plan?"

"I will, Madison. Thank you for your help. We will wait for an official determination of the fingerprint comparisons."

Joe looked at the faxed print card with the name Karter Truman on it and Truman's signature at the bottom. At the top of the card someone had stamped the NCIC fingerprint classification for Truman's prints. "FPC/ 19 PI PO PM 07 16 PO 18 PI CI"

Just as Joe hung up from his conversation with Madison the telephone rang again. Joe answered and listened to a man's voice.

"Sir, my name is Walter with the agency. With whom am I speaking?"

"This is Joe Creed."

"Is there a Casey Abbott available?"

"Yes sir. I will go get him."

Joe found Casey and told him of the waiting telephone call in Captain Fuerte's office.

A few minutes later, Casey returned to Joe and said, "Just as I finished my call, the phone rang again. Madison is waiting to speak with you."

"Hi, Joe, Madison here. The latent prints belong to Karter Truman, one hundred percent sure. I asked two different fingerprint specialists to check independently, and both confirmed you have Karter Truman's latent fingerprints. Would you let Marty know immediately?"

"Amazing! OK, I will let Marty know. Thank you, Madison. Talk to you later."

29.

MANTA

Captain Fuerte sent word out to the team to assemble in his office in 30 minutes for a conference call from Washington DC on the STU speaker telephone. The telephone rang and Captain Fuerte answered. A technician was on the other end and, after verifying the STU phone had been connected and was working correctly, turned the call over to Mr. Carlyle Maw.

"Greetings, my name is Carlyle Maw, and I am the Under Secretary of State for International Security Affairs. I have been directed by the President of the United States, and by the Honorable Henry Kissinger, Secretary of State, to co-chair an investigative and reactive body to identify the individuals and groups who have been engaged in a terrorist act of detonating a nuclear explosion on the southern border of the United States with México, and to extirpate the perpetrators. My co-chair will be Señor Hugo B. Maraqain, the Mexican ambassador to the United States. Members will include, but are not limited to, members of the: CIA, DEA, FBI, NSA, Armada de México Investigators, an Interpol representative, and a liaison to the United States Pentagon, including all of you listening on the speaker phone that have dealt with the threat up to this point. We shall call this task force the MANTA Team which stands for Mexican, American, Nuclear, Threat, Abatement Team. Any questions?"

"Joe Creed here, sir. I was wondering what the team's next move might be?"

"We are already moving on this abomination with everything we have. NSA, CIA, DEA, Mexican Investigators, Border Patrol, Interpol, have all been gathering information and evidence as we speak. After we debrief all of you, our next move will be to select a location for a physical meeting so that we can determine the mission's details and get moving on this action. I propose we organize as follows in the interest of economy and security. First, FBI Agent Madison Gardner will be the central repository of this mission's intelligence and information. All of you will have her toll-free telephone number. All investigators and members of the MANTA team will update Madison in a timely manner with information gathered so that she can process it and distribute it, as necessary, to mission members. In the interest of security, only those members with a need to know will receive updated information."

"Casey Abbott will manage SEAL Team 2, also known as Rat Pack, and SEAL team 4, known as Bigfoot, for missions yet to be determined. International insurance investigator Joe Creed and FBI Agent Marty Goodson will return to Yakima County and try to identify the person buried under the name Karter Truman. Marty and Joe will gather evidence showing Karter Truman is still alive if possible, and identify the body buried under his name. You both will then report to Washington DC for debriefings."

"The FBI director's aircraft will be used to transport all personnel associated with the previous missions to capture Nicholas Cabot and mitigate the nuclear threat at the border to the FBI headquarters in Washington DC for debriefings. Any questions? OK, since there are no questions, we will see you in Washington D.C."

"I'm sure looking forward to seeing Lydia, even though we still have plenty of work to do," Joe mentioned to Marty.

"We at least get a little family time before we have to go to Washington D.C. for the briefing. I think Buck, Annie and the SWAT guys will be happy to be back in the US," Marty responded.

"It will be good to see them. I wonder how Veronica is doing?" Joe asked as they walked to their quarters to prepare for the trip home.

"She is precious and needs to know how much we care for her. I will keep her informed as to Snake's memorial service," Joe remarked.

" I agree. We also need to find Karter Truman and shut his cartel friends down for good. I have a hunch it will take a coordinated effort for a considerable period of time to get the results we want," Marty commented.

"Home to Yakima. I can't wait to relax and snuggle with Lydia, after enjoying a nice meal, and the view of Mount Rainier and Mount Adams," Joe remarked.

EPILOGUE

The Grumman Gulfstream II jet made a quiet, quick, nighttime landing at the Tijuana México, General Ablardo L. Rodriguez International Airport on runway 27, and then taxied to the tarmac in front of the Mexican Navy Airbase hangar. Two Mexican sailors assisted in securing the aircraft and opening the door. FBI SWAT team members Hank Carter and Jack Rosen deplaned along with Hugo Chávez, Lieutenant Veronica Sabroso, and later FBI agents Annie Diaz, and Buck Buchanan. A meeting was called for all team members, including Bigfoot, Rat Pack, and all Mexican Navy Security personnel. The Mexican American Nuclear Threat Abatement team, (MANTA) composition and functions, along with individual mission plans were explained. The SWAT team members were ordered to return to their San Diego base, while most of the team, along with the Russian prisoner and cartel *sicario*, prepared to travel to Washington DC to be interrogated or debriefed.

At about the same time, in Phoenix, Arizona, Pedro Escobar waited with a Bonanno family member in a black Cadillac DeVille at Sky Harbor airport for a business jet to arrive from Teterboro, New Jersey. Pedro Escobar's suitcase was in the trunk of the Cadillac next to eleven, 50-pound packages stamped *"semillas vegetales"*. Another black Cadillac, occupied by four men dressed in dark suits, waited nearby while a Cessna Citation I business jet taxied towards them.

The Cessna Citation I, with its passenger and cargo labeled vegetable seeds, took off and headed to a meeting with family members in New York City.

About 30 minutes later the Grumman Gulfstream II left from Tijuana, routed first to Yakima for Joe and Marty, before going on to Washington DC with the remaining team members, a Russian meteorologist, and a cartel gunman.

It will be good to get back home with Lydia, Joe thought as he settled in for the return to Yakima.

Made in United States
Troutdale, OR
04/13/2024

19163845R00141